TM SERIES

Great Authors' Short Stories

COMPILED BY

PATRICIA MOORE

MG BOOKS

NEW DELHI (INDIA)

Great Authors' Short Stories

Published by

MG BOOKS

An Imprint of

MAANU GRAPHICS

MAANU GRAPHICS

(PUBLISHERS OF GENERAL BOOKS)

5FF, Ganpati Bhawan, 21 Ansari Road,
Darya Ganj, New Delhi-110002
Ph: 65285220, 64138266
E-mail : maanugraphics@yahoo.com
mgbooks.maanu@yahoo.com

Printed at
Satyam Enterprises, Delhi

CONTENTS

THE DANCING-PARTNER

– JEROME K. JEROME

'THIS story,' commenced macshaugnassy, 'comes from Furtwangen, a small town in the Black Forest. There lived there a very wonderful old fellow named Nicholau Geibel. His business was the making of mechanical toys, at which work he had aquired an almost European reputation. He made rabbits that would emerge from the heart of a cabbage, flop their ears, smooth their whiskers, and disappear again; cats that would wash their faces, and mew so naturally that dogs would mistake them for real cats, and fly at them; dolls, with phonographs concealed within them, that would raise their hats and say, "Good morning; how do you do?" and some that would even sing a song.

'But he was something more than a mere mechanic; he was an artist. His work was with him a hobby, almost a passion. His shop was filled with all manner of strange things that never would, or could, be sold, things he had made for the pure love of making them. He had contrived a mechanical donkey that would trot for two hours by means of stored electricity, and trot, too, much faster than the live article, and with less need for exertion on the part of the driver; a bird that would shoot up into the air, fly round and round in a circle, and drop to earth at the exact spot from where it started, a skeleton that, supported by an upright iron bar, would dance a hornpipe; a life-size lady doll that could play the fiddle; and a gentleman with a hollow inside who could smoke a pipe and drink more lager beer than any three average German students put together, which is saying much.

'Indeed, it was the belief of the town that old Geibel could make a man capable of doing everything that a respectable man need want to do. One day he made a man who did too much, and it came about in this way.

'Young Doctor Follen had a baby, and the baby had a birthday. Its first birthday put Doctor Follen's household into somewhat of a flurry, but on the occasion of its second birthday, Mrs Doctor Follen gave a ball in honour of the event. Old Geibel and his daughter Olga were among the guests.

'During the afternoon of the next day some three or four of Olga's bosom friends, who had also been present at the ball, dropped in to have a chat about it. They naturally fell to discussing the men, and to criticizing their dancing. Old Geibel was in the room, but he appeared to be absorbed in his newspaper, and the girls took no notice of him.

'"There seem to be fewer men who can dance at every ball you go to," said one of the girls.

'"Yes, and don't the ones who can, give themselves airs," said another, "they make quite a favour of asking you."

'"And how stupidly they talk," added a third. "They always say exactly the same things: 'How charming you are looking tonight.' 'Do you often go to Vienna? Oh, you should, it's delightful.' 'What a charming dress you have on.' 'What a warm day it has been.' 'Do you like Wagner?' I do wish they'd think of something new."

'"Oh, I never mind how they talk," said a fourth. "If a man dances well he may be a fool for all I care."

'"He generally is," slipped in a thin girl, rather spitefully.

'"I go to a ball to dance," continued the previous speaker, not noticing the interruption. "All I ask of a partner is that he shall hold me firmly, take me round steadily, and not get tired before I do."

'"A clockwork figure would be the thing for you," said the girl who had interrupted.

'"Bravo!" cried one of the others, clapping her hands, "what a capital idea!"

'"What's a capital idea?" they asked.

'"Why, a clockwork dancer, or, better still, one that would go by electricity and never run down."

'The girls took up the idea with enthusiasm.

'"Oh, what a lovely partner he would make," said one; "he would never kick you, or tread on your toes."

'"Or tear your dress," said another.

'"Or get out of step."

'"Or get giddy and lean on you."

"'And he would never want to mop his face with his handkerchief. I do hate to see a man do that after every dance."

'"And wouldn't want to spend the whole evening in the supper-room."

'"Why, with a phonograph inside him to grind out all the stock remarks, you would not be able to tell him from a real man," said the girl who had first suggested the idea.

'"Oh yes, you would," said the thin girl, "he would be so much nicer."

'Old Geibel had laid down his paper, and was listening with both his ears. On one of the girls glancing in his direction, however, he hurriedly hid himself again behind it.

'After the girls were gone, he went into his workshop, where Olga heard him walking up and down, and every now and then chuckling to himself; and that night he talked to her a good deal about dancing and dancing men - asked what they usually said and did - what dances were most popular - what steps were gone through, with many other questions bearing on the subject.

'Then for a couple of weeks he kept much to his factory, and was very thoughtful and busy, though prone at unexpected moments to break into a quiet low laugh, as if enjoying a joke that nobody else knew of.

'A month later another ball took place in Furtwangen. On this occasion it was given by old Wenzel, the wealthy timber merchant, to celebrate his niece's betrothal, and Geibel and his daughter were again among the invited.

'When the hour arrived to set out, Olga sought her father. Not finding him in the house, she tapped at the door of his workshop. He appeared in his shirt-sleeves, looking hot but radiant.

'"Don't wait for me," he said, "you go on. I'll follow you. I've got something to finish."

'As she turned to obey he called after her. "Tell them I'm going to bring a young man with me - such a nice young man, and an excellent dancer. All the girls will like him." Then he laughed and closed the door.

'Her father generally kept his doings secret from everybody, but she had a pretty shrewd suspicion of what he had been planning, and so, to a certain extent, was able to prepare the guests for what was coming. Anticipation ran high, and the arrival of the famous mechanist was eagerly awaited.

'At length the sound of wheels was heard outside, followed by a great commotion in the passage, and old Wenzel himself, his jolly face red with excitement and suppressed laughter, burst into the room and announced in stentorian tones:

'"Herr Geibel - and a friend."

'Herr Geibel and his "friend" entered, greeted with shouts of laughter and applause, and advanced to the centre of the room.

'"Allow me, ladies and gentlemen," said Herr Geibel, "to introduce you to my friend, Lieutenant Fritz. Fritz, my dear fellow, bow to the ladies and gentlemen."

'Geibel placed his hand encouragingly on Fritz's shoulder, and the lieutenant bowed low, accompanying the action with a harsh clicking noise in his throat, unpleasantly suggestive of a death rattle. But that was only a detail.

'"He walks a little stiffly" (old Geibel took his arm and walked him forward a few steps. He certainly did walk stiffly), "but then walking is not his forte. He is essentially a dancing man. I have only been able to teach him the waltz as yet, but at that he is faultless. Come, which of you ladies may I introduce him to as a partner? He keeps perfect time; he never gets tired; he won't kick you or tread on your dress; he will hold you as firmly as you like, and go as quickly or as slowly as you please; he never gets giddy; and he is full of conversation. Come, speak up for yourself, my boy."

'The old gentleman twisted one of the buttons at the back of his coat, and immediately Fritz opened his mouth, and in thin tones that appeared to proceed from the back of his head, remarked suddenly, "May I have the pleasure?" and then shut his mouth again with a snap.

'That Lieutenant Fritz had made a strong impression on the company was undoubted, yet none of the girls seemed inclined to dance with him. They looked askance at his waxen face, with its staring eyes and fixed smile, and shuddered. At last old Geibel came to the girl who had conceived the idea.

'"It is your own suggestion, carried out to the letter," said Geibel, "an electric dancer. You owe it to the gentleman to give him a trial."

'She was a bright, saucy little girl, fond of a frolic. Her host added his entreaties, and she consented.

'Herr Geibel fixed the figure to her. Its right arm was screwed round her waist, and held her firmly; its delicately jointed left hand was made to fasten itself upon her right. The old toy-maker showed her how to regulate its speed, and how to stop it, and release her.

'"It will take you round in a complete circle," he explained, "be careful that no one knocks against you, and alters its course."

The music struck up. Old Geibel put the current in motion, and Annette and her strange partner began to dance.

'For a while everyone stood watching them. The figure performed its purpose admirably. Keeping perfect time and step, and holding its little partner tight clasped in an unyielding embrace, it revolved steadily, pouring forth at the same time a constant flow of squeaky conversation, broken by brief intervals of grinding silence.

'"How charming you are looking tonight," it remarked in its thin, faraway voice. "What a lovely day it has been. Do you like dancing? How well our steps agree. You will give me another, won't you? Oh, don't be so cruel. What a charming gown you have on. Isn't waltzing delightful? I could go on dancing for ever - with you. Have you had supper?"

'As she grew more familiar with the uncanny creature, the girl's nervousness wore off, and she entered into the fun of the thing.

'"Oh, he's just lovely," she cried, laughing, "I could go on dancing with him all my life."

'Couple after couple now joined them, and soon all the dancers in the room were whirling round behind them. Nicholau Geibel stood looking on, beaming with childish delight at his success.

'Old Wenzel approached him, and whispered something in his ear. Geibel laughed and nodded, and the two worked their way quietly towards the door.

'"This is the young people's house tonight," said Wenzel, so soon as they were outside; "you and I will have a quiet pipe and a glass of hock, over in the counting-house."

'Meanwhile the dancing grew more fast and furious. Little Annette loosened the screw regulating her partner's rate of progress, and the figure flew round with her, swifter and swifter. Couple after couple dropped out exhausted, but they only went the faster, till at length they remained dancing alone.

'Madder and madder became the waltz. The music lagged behind: the musicians, unable to keep pace, ceased, and sat staring. The younger guests applauded, but the older faces began to grow anxious.

'"Hadn't you better stop, dear?" said one of the women. "You'll make yourself so tired."

'But Annette did not answer.

'"I believe she's fainted," cried out a girl who had caught sight of her face as it was swept by.

'One of the men sprang forward and clutched at the figure, but its impetus threw him down on to the floor, where its steel-cased feet laid bare his cheek. The thing evidently did not intend to part with its prize easily.

'Had anyone retained a cool head, the figure, one cannot help thinking, might easily have been stopped. Two or three men acting in concert might have lifted it bodily off the floor, or have jabbed it into a corner. But few human heads are capable of remaining cool under excitement. Those who are not present think how stupid must have been those who were; those who are reflect afterwards how simple it would have been to do this, that, or the other, if only they had thought of it at the time.

'The women grew hysterical. The men shouted contradictory directions to one another. Two of them made a bungling rush at the figure, which had the result of forcing it out of its orbit in the centre of the room, and sending it crashing against the walls and furniture. A stream of blood showed itself down the girl's white frock, and followed her along the floor. The affair was becoming horrible. The women rushed screaming from the room. The men followed them.

'One sensible suggestion was made: "Find Geibel - fetch Geibel."

'No one had noticed him leave the room, no one knew where he was. A party went in search of him. The others, too unnerved to go back into the ball-room, crowded outside the door and listened. They could hear the steady whir of the wheels upon the polished floor as the thing spun round and round; the dull thud as every now and again it dashed itself and its burden against some opposing object and ricocheted off in a new direction.

'And everlastingly it talked in that thin ghostly voice, repeating over and over the same formula: "How charming you are looking tonight. What a lovely day it has been. Oh, don't be so cruel. I could go on dancing for ever - with you. Have you had supper?"

'Of course they sought for Geibel everywhere but where he was. They looked in every room in the house, then they rushed off in a body to his own place, and spent precious minutes in waking up his deaf old housekeeper. At last it occurred to one of the party that Wenzel was missing also, and then the idea of the counting-house across the yard presented itself to them, and there they found him.

'He rose up, very pale, and followed them; and he and old Wenzel forced their way through the crowd of guests gathered outside, and entered the room, and locked the door behind them.

'From within there came the muffled sound of low voices and quick steps, followed by a confused scuffling noise, then silence, then the low voices again.

'After a time the door opened, and those near it pressed forward to enter, but old Wenzel's broad shoulders barred the way.

'"I want you - and you, Bekler," he said, addressing a couple of the older men. His voice was calm, but his face was deadly white. "The rest of you, please go - get the women away as quickly as you can."

'From that day old Nicholau Geibel confined himself to the making of mechanical rabbits, and cats that mewed and washed their faces.'

ALL CREATURES GREAT AND SMALL

– JAMES HERRIOT

***

THEY didn't say anything about this in the books, I thought, as the snow blew in through the gaping doorway and settled on my naked back.

I lay face down on the cobbled floor in a pool of nameless muck, my arm deep inside the straining cow, my feet scrabbling for a toe hold between the stones. I was stripped to the waist and the snow mingled with the dirt and the dried blood on my body. I could see nothing outside the circle of flickering light thrown by the smoky oil lamp which the farmer held over me.

No, there wasn't a word in the books about searching for your ropes and instruments in the shadows; about trying to keep clean in a half bucket of tepid water; about the cobbles digging into your chest. Nor about the slow numbing of the arms, the creeping paralysis of the muscles as the fingers tried to work against the cow's powerful expulsive efforts.

There was no mention anywhere of the gradual exhaustion, the feeling of futility and the little far-off voice of panic.

My mind went back to that picture in the obstetrics book. A cow standing in the middle of a gleaming floor while a sleek veterinary surgeon in a spotless parturition overall inserted his arm to a polite distance. He was relaxed and smiling, the farmer and his helpers were smiling, even the cow was smiling. There was no dirt or blood or sweat anywhere.

That man in the picture had just finished an excellent lunch and had moved next door to do a bit of calving just for the sheer pleasure of it, as a kind of dessert. He hadn't crawled shivering from his bed at two o'clock in the morning and bumped over twelve miles of frozen snow, staring sleepily ahead till the lonely farm showed in the headlights. He hadn't climbed half a mile of white fellside to the doorless barn where his patient lay.

I tried to wriggle my way an extra inch inside the cow. The calf's head was back and I was painfully pushing a thin, looped rope towards its lower jaw with my finger tips. All the time my arm was being squeezed between the calf and the bony pelvis. With every straining effort from the cow the pressure became almost unbearable, then she would relax and I would push the rope another inch. I wondered how long I would be able to keep this up. If I didn't snare that jaw soon I would never get the calf away. I groaned, set my teeth and reached forward again.

Another little flurry of snow blew in and I could almost hear the flakes sizzling on my sweating back. There was sweat on my forehead too, and it trickled into my eyes as I pushed.

There is always a time at a bad calving when you begin to wonder if you will ever win the battle. I had reached this stage.

Little speeches began to flit through my brain. 'Perhaps it would be better to slaughter this cow. Her pelvis is so small and narrow that I can't see a calf coming through', or 'She's a good fat animal and really of the beef type, so don't you think it would pay you better to get the butcher?' or perhaps This is a very bad presentation. In a roomy cow it would be simple enough to bring the head round but in this case it is just about impossible.'

Of course, I could have delivered the calf by embryotomy - by passing a wire over the neck and sawing off the head. So many of these occasions ended with the floor strewn with heads, legs, heaps of intestines. There were thick textbooks devoted to the countless ways you could cut up a calf.

But none of it was any good here, because this calf was alive. At my furthest stretch I had got my finger as far as the commissure of the mouth and had been startled by a twitch of the little creature's tongue. It was unexpected because calves in this position are usually dead, asphyxiated by the acute flexion of the neck and the pressure of the dam's powerful contractions. But this one had a spark of life in it and if it came out it would have to be in one piece.

I went over to my bucket of water, cold now and bloody, and silently soaped my arms. Then I lay down again, feeling the cobbles harder than ever against my chest. I worked my toes between the stones, shook the sweat from my eyes and for the hundredth time thrust an arm that felt like spaghetti into the cow; alongside the little dry legs of the calf, like sandpaper tearing against my flesh, then to the bend in the neck and so to the ear and then, agonizingly, along the side of the face towards the lower jaw which had become my major goal in life.

It was incredible that I had been doing this for nearly two hours; fighting as my strength ebbed to push a little noose round that jaw. I had tried everything else - repelling a leg, gentle traction with a blunt hook in the eye socket, but I was back to the noose.

It had been a miserable session all through. The farmer, Mr Dinsdale, was a long, sad, silent man of few words who always seemed to be expecting the worst to happen. He had a long, sad, silent son with him and the two of them had watched my efforts with deepening gloom.

But worst of all had been Uncle. When I had first entered the hillside barn I had been surprised to see a little bright-eyed old man in a pork pie hat settling down comfortably on a bale of straw. He was filling his pipe and clearly looking forward to the entertainment.

'Now then, young man,' he cried in the nasal twang of the West Riding. 'I'm Mr Dinsdale's brother. I farm over in Listondale.'

I put down my equipment and nodded. 'How do you do? My name is Herriot.'

The old man looked me over, piercingly. 'My vet is Mr Broomfield. Expect you'll have heard of him - everybody knows him, I reckon. Wonderful man, Mr Broomfield, especially at calving. Do you know, I've never seen 'im beat yet.'

I managed a wan smile. Any other time I would have been delighted to hear how good my colleague was, but somehow not now, not now. In fact, the words set a mournful little bell tolling inside me.

'No, I'm afraid I don't know Mr Broomfield,' I said, taking off my jacket and, more reluctantly, peeling my shirt over my head. 'But I haven't been around these parts very long.'

Uncle was aghast. 'You don't know him! Well you're the only one as doesn't. They think the world of him in Listondale, I can tell you.' He lapsed into a shocked silence and applied a match to his pipe. Then he shot a glance at my goose-pimpled torso. 'Strips like a boxer does Mr Broomfleld. Never seen such muscles on a man.'

A wave of weakness coursed sluggishly over me. I felt suddenly leaden-footed and inadequate. As I began to lay out my ropes and instruments on a clean towel the old man spoke again.

'And how long have you been qualified, may I ask?'

'Oh, about seven months.'

'Seven months!' Uncle smiled indulgently, tamped down his tobacco and blew out a cloud of rank, blue smoke. 'Well, there's nowt like a bit of experience, I always says. Mr Broomfield's been doing my work now for over ten years and he really knows what he's about. No, you can 'ave your book learning. Give me experience every time.'

I tipped some antiseptic into the bucket and lathered my arms carefully. I knelt behind the cow.

'Mr Broomfield always puts some special lubricating oils on his arms first,' Uncle said, pulling contentedly on his pipe. 'He says you get infection of the womb if you just use soap and water.'

I made my first exploration. It was the burdened moment all vets go through when they first put their hand into a cow. Within seconds I would know whether I would be putting on my jacket in fifteen minutes or whether I had hours of hard labour ahead of me.

I was going to be unlucky this time; it was a nasty presentation. Head back and no room at all; more like being inside an undeveloped heifer than a second calver. And she was bone dry - the 'waters' must have come away from her hours ago. She had been running out on the high fields and had started to calve a week before her time; that was why they had had to bring her into this half-ruined barn. Anyway, it would be a long time before I saw my bed again.

'Well now, what have you found, young man?' Uncle's penetrating voice cut through the silence. 'Head back, eh? You won't have much trouble, then. I've seen Mr Broomfield do 'em like that - he turns calf right round and brings it out back legs first.'

I had heard this sort of nonsense before. A short time in practice had taught me that all farmers were experts with other farmers' livestock. When their own animals were in trouble they tended to rush to the phone for the vet, but with their neighbours' they were confident, knowledgeable and full of helpful advice. And another phenomenon I had observed was that their advice was usually regarded as more valuable than the vet's. Like now, for instance, Uncle was obviously an accepted sage and the Dinsdales listened with deference to everything he said.

'Another way with a job like this,' continued Uncle, 'is to get a few strong chaps with ropes and pull the thing out, head back and all.'

I gasped as I felt my way around. 'I'm afraid it's impossible to turn a calf completely round in this small space. And to pull it out without bringing the head round would certainly break the mother's pelvis.'

The Dinsdales narrowed their eyes. Clearly they thought I was hedging in the face of Uncle's superior knowledge.

And now, two hours later, defeat was just round the corner. I was just about whacked. I had rolled and grovelled on the filthy cobbles while the Dinsdales watched me in morose silence and Uncle kept up a non-stop stream of comment. Uncle, his ruddy face glowing with delight, his little eyes sparkling, hadn't had such a happy night for years. His long trek up the hillside had been repaid a hundredfold. His vitality was undiminished; he had enjoyed every minute.

As I lay there, eyes closed, face stiff with dirt, mouth hanging open, Uncle took his pipe in his hand and leaned forward on his straw bale. 'You're about beat, young man,' he said with deep satisfaction. 'Well, I've never seen Mr Broomfield beat but he's had a lot of experience. And what's more, he's strong, really strong. That's one man you couldn't tire.'

Rage flooded through me like a draught of strong spirit. They right thing to do, of course, would be to get up, tip the bucket of bloody water over Uncle's head, run down the hill and drive away; away from Yorkshire, from Uncle, from the Dinsdales, from this cow.

Instead, I clenched my teeth, braced my legs and pushed with everything I had; and with a sensation of disbelief I felt my noose slide over the sharp little incisor teeth and into the calf's mouth. Gingerly, muttering a prayer, I pulled on the thin rope with my left hand and felt the slipknot tighten. I had hold of that lower jaw.

At last I could start doing something. 'Now hold this rope, Mr Dinsdale, and just keep a gentle tension on it. I'm going to repel the calf and if you pull steadily at the same time, the head ought to come round.'

'What if the rope comes off?' asked Uncle hopefully.

I didn't answer. I put my hand in against the calf's shoulder and began to push against the cow's contractions. I felt the small body moving away from me. 'Now a steady pull, Mr Dinsdale, without jerking.' And to myself, 'Oh God, don't let it slip off.'

The head was coming round. I could feel the neck straightening against my arm, then the ear touched my elbow. I let go the shoulder and grabbed the little muzzle. Keeping the teeth away from the vaginal wall with my hand, I guided the head till it was resting where it should be, on the fore limbs.

Quickly I extended the noose till it reached behind the ears. 'Now pull on the head as she strains.'

'Nay, you should pull on the legs now,' cried Uncle.

'Pull on the bloody head rope, I tell you!' I bellowed at the top of my voice and felt immediately better as Uncle retired, offended, to his bale.

With traction the head was brought out and the rest of the body followed easily. The little animal lay motionless on the cobbles, eyes glassy and unseeing, tongue blue and grossly swollen.

'It'll be dead. Bound to be,' grunted Uncle, returning to the attack.

I cleared the mucus from the mouth, blew hard down the throat and began artificial respiration. After a few pressures on the ribs, the calf gave a gasp and the eyelids flickered. Then it started to inhale and one leg jerked.

Uncle took off his hat and scratched his head in disbelief. 'By gaw, it's alive. I'd have thowt it'd sure to be dead after you'd messed about all that time.' A lot of the fire had gone out of him and his pipe hung down empty from his lips.

'I know what this little fellow wants,' I said. I grasped the calf by its fore legs and pulled it up to its mother's head. The cow was stretched out on her side, her head extended wearily along the rough floor. Her ribs heaved, her eyes were almost closed, she looked past caring about anything. Then she felt the calf's body against her face and there was a transformation; her eyes opened wide and her muzzle began a snuffling exploration of the new object. Her interest grew with every sniff and she struggled on to her chest, nosing and probing all over the calf, rumbling deep in her chest. Then she began to lick him methodically. Nature provides the perfect stimulant massage for a time like this and the little creature arched his back as the coarse papillae on the tongue dragged along his skin. Within a minute he was shaking his head and trying to sit up.

I grinned. This was the bit I liked. The little miracle. I felt it was something that would never grow stale no matter how often I saw it. I cleaned as much of the dried blood and filth from my body as I could, but most of it had caked on my skin and not even my finger nails would move it. It would have to wait for the hot bath at home. Pulling my shirt over my head, I felt as though I had been beaten for a long time with a thick stick. Every muscle ached. My mouth was dried out, my lips almost stieking together.

A long, sad figure hovered near. 'How about a drink?' asked Mr Dinsdale.

I could feel my grimy face cracking into an incredulous smile. A vision of hot tea well laced with whisky swam before me. 'That's very kind of you, Mr Dinsdale, I'd love a drink. It's been a hard two hours.'

'Nay,' said Mr Dinsdale looking at me steadily, 'I meant for the cow.'

I began to babble. 'Oh yes, of course, certainly, by all means give her a drink. She must be very thirsty. It'll do her good. Certainly, certainly, give her a drink.'

I gathered up my tackle and stumbled out of the barn. On the moor it was still dark and a bitter wind whipped over the snow, stinging my eyes. As I plodded down the slope, Uncle's voice, strident and undefeated, reached me for the last time.

'Mr Broomfield doesn't believe in giving a drink after calving. Says it chills the stomach.'

DOCTOR ZEIT

– ANTONIA FRASER

'I'M being pursued by this face; she thought. This old face. I'm frightened. I'll have to do something.'

The first time Nola saw the face she was in the underground, on the moving stairs coming up to the Tottenham Court Road. The last leg of the journey. Nola always felt like a seal coming up for air at Tottenham Court Road tube with its double staircase. She began to breathe deeply as she reached the top. Nola was not particularly strong and she felt she needed all the air she could get before she reached the British Museum, and the somewhat airless atmosphere of its Reading Room.

Nola had been working for the past two years on a study of seventeenth-century family life. She still had a long way to go. From time to time she told her publisher, lightly, that twentieth-century family life came first. Which meant the house in Islington with the lovely wooden polished floors, kitchen often full of healthy foods, large country-style garden - all of them rivals for her attention with the British Museum.

And, of course, there were Denis and Johnnie. Denis was Nola's husband and Johnnie was her son. To Nola, privately, they were the perfect family unit. She had no wish for another child. Denis protected Nola - he was much older than her - and Nola protected Johnnie. Indeed, when she thought about Johnnie's small but perfectly male body, Nola imagined that she felt the same joy that Denis often told her he felt in her youth, her beauty (because of the difference in their ages, he said, to him she would always look young, no matter how the years passed).

On her route to and from the British Museum. Nola's favourite thoughts were of the two of them. She was meditating on Johnnie and how perfect he was, and how in a way she wished he could stay five years old forever, so gay, so ebullient, so amusing, so much her little boy ... when she felt a slight tug on her long skirt. Nola turned round. The staircase was not particularly crowded - it was after ten o'clock and the workers had vanished to their offices. Several steps below her a woman with a very old face was smiling at her. At least Nola thought at the time that she was a woman, but she was so very old, judging from her face at least, that she had already reached that stage of asexuality of appearance which makes it difficult to tell the inhabitants of male and female geriatric wards apart.

Nola had certainly never seen the woman before in her life. Nola presumed therefore that she had dropped something. But her bag was standing neatly intact on the step above her. She checked it, looked round again, missed the old woman completely, found the top of the staircase claiming her attention, searched for her ticket and furgot the incident.

The second time that Nola saw the face, it was definitely on a man. On him - that was how she instinctively put it to herself because despite the fact that the face was exactly the same as the previous face, old, really old, seamily wrinkled flesh hanging round the jowls, wispy hair, she got the odd impression that she was not seeing the same person so much as the same face.

On this occasion she saw the face and its bearer standing on the platform of Tottenham Court Road tube station as her train drew in. She had a quick uncomfortable flash of recognition and the face -the man rather - seemed to feel likewise because he gave a little salute with his hand. The other hand held a stick. When Nola got off the train, he was gone. He had presumably entered the train elsewhere where it was less crowded.

The third occasion she saw the face was more disturbing. It was Johnnie's half term. Nola had a choice of staying at home with him or taking him along with her, since Denis was, of course, at the office. She decided to take him on a visit to the British Museum.

Not into the Reading Room, of course; that was out of the question, perish the thought of introducing rumbustious Johnnie into such a sanctum even if it had been permitted. But she did think it would be rather pleasant to show Johnnie some of the sights, the Elgin Marbles, vast sphinxes, statues, the sort of thing that an intelligent five year old would find quite stimulating to the imagination without precisely understanding them. And she would point to the door of the Reading Room, perhaps, and call it 'Mum's office'. Johnnie knew about offices. He had visited Denis' office on several occasions. When Denis returned in the evening, Johnnie used to chant: 'Back from the office' as if it was all one word. They set off early so as to be back for Johnnie's lunch.

But Johnnie and Nola never got as far as the British Museum. At Tottenham Court Road station (This is where Mum comes to work in the morning'), the most awful thing happened. Johnnie disappeared. One moment he was holding Nola's hand, the next moment there was a sharp tug and he was gone. Through the pressing crowd, he vanished completely. Nola was distraught, sick with fear.

'Johnnie, Johnnie,' she screamed, turning round and trying to battle her way against the incoming crowd.

She struggled back finally onto the platform from whence they had come. And saw two things. Johnnie, tearful, holding the hand of a black Underground Inspector, who was bending down and trying to comfort him. For a split second she also saw that face, that old face. She would know it anywhere. But this time on quite a young and sturdy body; she had the impression of jeans, a tee-shirt. The man, woman, whatever it was, smiled and vanished down the far exit to the other line.

Johnnie, sobbing, seemed to expect Nola to punish him. In self-defence he talked of a horrible old man with a nasty smell pulling him away.

'I couldn't help it. He was much stronger than me,' he kept saying. 'Darling, we're going straight home,' was all Nola could bring herself to reply.

When she told Denis about it in the evening - an edited version not mentioning the previous encounters with the face - he said quite sharply:

'Wasn't it rather silly to take a kid to the BM in the first place? I mean, you can go there as much as you like when he's at school. I shouldn't think it would have been quite his cup of tea if you had got there. He's still at the playground stage if you ask me.'

Nola, feeling guilty, forbore to mention her plan of showing the door of 'Mum's office'. Denis was right. Johnnie had not yet reached the sightseeing stage: she was the one who did not want him to grow up too fast, and now she was trying to force the pace.

The fourth, fifth and sixth times Nola saw the face were in and around Islington when she was shopping or on her way to fetch Johnnie from school. On each occasion the face smiled at her. Johnnie was right: it was definitely an old man. The impression of a youthful body and jeans that day must have been part of her general distraction at losing the child. The truth was, she told herself, that he was just a rather mad old man who happened to live in Islington and filled in the time leering at young women ... Perfectly harmless if unpleasant. Nola pulled herself up: not *totally* harmless, if her theory was correct. The old man had tried to kidnap Johnnie. No, that was really going much too far in the other direction. Kidnap was far too strong a word. Denis had been quite right when he pointed out that Johnnie was only a child, had been known to wriggle his hand free under other circumstances.

'Probably just didn't want to go to the BM,' said Denis with a smile. He worried a little all the same - not about Johnnie but about Nola. Nola, of all the women he knew, was the most conscientious mother. And wife. And then there was her book. And her health. Health, which was never strong and could too easily lead to nervousness and collapse if Nola overstretched herself. However, Denis and Nola had agreed long ago when they first married never to refer to Nola's condition and to live their lives exactly as if it did not exist. So Denis decided to say nothing more on this occasion, only to watch Nola more carefully in future. At least he could try and see that she did not overdo the British Museum stuff.

But, of course, Nola's projected book had to have its place in her life, along with the house and the garden and the creative kitchen and Denis and Johnnie. The idea had originated as a post-graduate thesis suggested by Nola's tutor, who had a high opinion of her work. It was a task to which marriage to Denis and the birth of Johnnie put an end. Only temporarily, however. Nola got back to it once Johnnie went to nursery school. And it was really much more fun doing it in terms of a proper book, being her own mistress as it were, without the inevitable restraints of the structure of a thesis. Besides which she no longer needed a grant to support herself while working on it.

'You're my grant,' she told Denis. 'And a very nice grant too.'

If Nola's progress was slow - school holidays were an

interruption - at least it was steady. And she never found any difficulty in picking up her work again where she had left off: the mere entry into the atmosphere of the Reading Room, airless as it might be, transported her. It was in its own way like a Secret Garden to which Nola - and admittedly five hundred others - had the key.

So it was fantastically upsetting one morning, as she arrived later than her schedule, to see the face, sitting three along from the seat she usually occupied. Not in her seat, thank God, that would have been too much; might have persuaded her she was seeing an apparition, a sort of doppelganger, an aged version of herself - but she wasn't seeing an apparition, she knew that. This old woman -and she was definitely a woman this time - was real. What was more, as Nola flung down her bag on her seat, the woman with the old face got up and shuffled off in the direction of the North Library. The old face did not smile, Nola noticed, there was a nasty set grumpy look about it, the mouth above the hanging dewlaps. On the whole, however, Nola preferred this air of crossness even anger to the original leer. Besides which the old woman had left her books behind on the table. Nola could see them lying there.

Now was her chance to find out a little more about her pursuer. With a feeling of determination, Nola strode down the row of desks and picked up the book lying open. She nearly dropped it with surprise. It was Levin Schucking's Puritan Family. It was a comparatively new book which had come out since Nola began working on her subject and Nola had made quite a bit of use of it herself. She did not know why she was so surprised at the sight of it on the old woman's desk. It was a most disagreeable sensation.

Still more disagreeable, was the discovery that the other four books on the desk were all pertaining to the subject of women and marriage in the seventeenth-century - or as you might put it, seventeenth-century family life. Some of them were quite obscure.

Nola took a decision. She put in a slip for Schucking's book, and duly got her slip returned with the scribbled information on the back that it was 'Out to another reader': she could not quite read it but the name looked like Zett. Nola went to the centre desk and explained her problem.

'The old lady who has it out was sitting quite close to me as a matter of fact. But she went out an hour ago and hasn't returned. So I wondered if I could just check something . . .'

'Name?' said the man behind the desk with professional politeness but without interest.

'Zett, it looks like, or Zeit.'

The man's face clouded.

'Oh dear. Old Mrs Zeit. Or rather Frau Doktor Zeit as she prefers to be called. Oh dear. Well, I'll see what I can do when she comes back.'

'Is she - er?' Nola pursued delicately, prompting, not finishing the sentence. The man grinned and raised his eyebrows. She saw that he was quite young.

'Shall we say that she's a little difficult?' he said. 'We get them in here. Delusions of persecution. Probably a refugee from somewhere. She thinks everyone is trying to steal her researches from her before she can write her book —'

'And her book is on —?'

The young man took thought.

'Seventeenth-century family life,' he answered. 'Something like that.'

He was surprised when Nola, who had seemed such a pleasant person, turned on her heel abruptly and marched out of the Reading Room. Actually Nola was going to the Ladies because she felt dizzy. And when she came back she just collected her bag and left. Frau Doktor Zeit was not there. All the same, she knew she could not do any work that day.

This was the point at which Nola thought: '*I'm* being pursued by this face. This old face. I'm frightened. I shall have to do something.'

She told Denis that she had discovered an old woman in the Reading Room who was working on exactly the same subject as herself - and for a book, too; she felt that it was a catastrophe. That was as far as Nola could bring herself to relate recent events for the time being. If Denis were sympathetic - and she knew he would be - she could probably nerve herself to discuss the face itself thereafter.

'Don't go to the British Museum, darling, for a bit,' said Denis immediately. 'You've had a shock. I can see that. Not that some old crone "is really going to write a book and steal your thunder. Not a chance. Your book will be terrific when it comes out, never fear. But the truth is you've been overdoing it lately. A rest - here at home -will freshen you up. Work twice as hard when you get back to it.'

'I've got so much to get through,' Nola began rather

desperately. Denis soothed her. 'Darling, I know.'

'But the time's passing –'

'There's plenty of time. For one thing Johnnie won't be a baby forever. He won't need fetching and carrying from school forever.'

'And I suppose you're going to grow out of needing a hot dinner at night,' said Nola wryly.

'Exactly,' Denis beamed. 'My teeth will soon fall out. Then I shan't be able to eat anything but cereal. That means you won't have to cook at all.'

Nola looked worried again. 'Don't talk like that,' she begged. 'On top of everything else. You know I can't bear to think of you getting old.'

It was the solitary hang-up she had about the disparity in their ages. She could not bear a mention of such things, even a light reflexion like the fact that Denis would be sixty-five and retiring when Johnnie was twenty one and going out to work, caused her to shiver.

'Now Nola,' said Denis, taking her in his arms. 'You really are out to upset yourself, aren't you? As for me, I'm in the pink of health. I had the firm's annual medical check-up today. I forgot to tell you with all this going on. I'm A 1. OK the doctor told me. The physique of a young man. Not so the doctor himself, I must say. Talking of the old, this was the oldest fellow I have ever seen. I thought I must have made a mistake when I stepped into the consulting room. He looked just like a tortoise.'

'A man with a very old face?' Nola asked carefully, after a pause.

'That's right. He might have been Methuselah himself. But he gave me a clean bill of health. Wait a moment, darling. I'm crazy. You know him. When I said goodbye, he asked me to give you his love. You and Johnnie. But especially you. He's an Austrian. Doctor Zeit, I think his name was - Why darling.'

As Denis held Nola, he felt her go slack and heavy in his arms. She had fainted.

'It was nothing,' said Nola a minute later when she found herself sitting on the sofa. 'Just one of my turns. Don't fuss me You promised.' She saw Denis' anxious face leaning over her and went on: 'Don't worry . . .' It was like when they were first married. Her one concern was to reassure him about her.

But Denis did worry. Despite Nola's protests, he insisted on putting her to bed for the rest of the evening. In return, he promised not to fuss her too much the next day.

Nevertheless, Nola did not even try to go to the British Museum. She did not feel up to it. And she kept Johnnie at home, too, although Denis did not know that till later. He generally left for the office before Johnnie went to school. All the same Nola was determined not to waste the day entirely. She pondered between the rival claims of kitchen and garden A day cooking for the deep freeze? Or a day really tidying up the garden before the onset of winter? In the end the garden won, because Nola had to admit that the garden was showing signs of positive neglect whereas the kitchen wasn't. When Denis telephoned her later that morning, ostensibly to consult her about an invitation, Nola told him:

'By the way, I'm clearing up the garden. It's rather fun.'

'Just the ticket.' Denis managed to sound delighted. 'It's a beautiful day for it too. I walked half the way to the office.'

Nola dug a little, created a pile of rubbish and finally went indoors with the laudable intention of doing to the airing cupboard what she had just done for the garden. She was upstairs on a ladder, reaching tor the back of the cupboard when she heard the front door bell ring. Nola hesitated and looked at Johnnie.

'Johnnie, could you?'

''Course I could,' he said contemptuously. Later Johnnie shouted something up the stairs about the garden. Nola was rather puzzled. She ought really to go down - but Johnnie had panted back up the stairs again.

'Daddy sent someone to do the garden for you. So I let him through the back door,' he said importantly.

'Oh I see.' Nola was taken aback and suddenly rather chilled. Hadn't she been going to do the garden herself? Denis was treating her like a baby again, not wanting her to strain herself.

Presently Nola looked out of the window and saw the gardener's back. He was wearing jeans and to her surprise he appeared to be wielding a scythe. She looked again. Yes, it was definitely a scythe. In their garden and at this time of year! What was Denis thinking of?

Johnnie was in his room, playing with his little cars in the window seat. Nola gave him a quick glance and then clattered down the stairs and into the garden.

'Excuse me,' she said in a voice of authority. 'What are you doing with that scythe?' The young man stood up and turned round. He was still holding his scythe as he moved towards Nola. His voice was quite young and musical when he replied:

'I'm caring for your garden. Don't worry. I shall be here to care for it after you are gone.'

But his face was an old face, a familiar face.

Johnnie, looking out of the window, saw his mother fall down and lie still. Later he described to his father exactly the man who had come to do the garden, the man with the scythe, in jeans, but a man with a terribly old face. He told his father that the man with the terribly old face had cut down his mother with his scythe. But that was nonsense, of course; a child's reaction to shock. There was not a mark on Nola's body.

THE NEW GIRLFRIEND

– RUTH RENDELL

'YOU know what we did last time?' he said.

She had waited for this for weeks. 'Yes?'

'I wondered if you'd like to do it again.'

She longed to but she didn't want to sound too keen. 'Why not?'

'How about Friday afternoon then? I've got the day off and Angie always goes to her sister's on Friday.'

'Not always, David.' She giggled.

He also laughed a little. 'She will this week. Do you think we could use your car? Angie'll take ours.'

'Of course. I'll come for you about two, shall I?'

'I'll open the garage doors and you can drive straight in. Oh, and Chris, could you fix it to get back a bit later? I'd love it if we could have the whole evening together.'

'I'll try,' she said, and then, 'I'm sure I can fix it. I'll tell Graham I'm going out with my new girl friend.'

He said good-bye and that he would see her on Friday. Christine put the receiver back. She had almost given up expecting a call from him. But there must have been a grain of hope still, for she had never left the receiver off the way she used to.

The last time she had done that was on a Thursday three weeks before, the day she had gone round to Angie's and found David there alone. Christine had got into the habit of taking the phone off the hook during the middle part of the day to avoid getting calls for the Midland Bank. Her number and the Midland Bank's differed by only one digit. Most days she took the receiver off at nine-thirty and put it back at three-thirty. On Thursday afternoons she nearly always went round to see Angie and never bothered to phone first.

Christine knew Angie's husband quite well. If she stayed a bit later on Thursdays she saw him when he came home from work. Sometimes she and Graham and Angie and David went out together as a foursome. She knew that David, like Graham, was a salesman or sales executive, as Graham always described himself, and she guessed from her friend's lifestyle that David was rather more successful at it. She had never found him particularly attractive, for, although he was quite tall, he had something of a girlish look and very fair wavy hair.

Graham was a heavily-built, very dark man with a swarthy skin. He had to shave twice a day. Christine had started going out with him when she was fifteen and they had got married on her eighteenth birthday. She had never really known any other men at all intimately and now if she ever found herself alone with a man she felt awkward and apprehensive. The truth was that she was afraid a man might make an advance to her and the thought of that frightened her very much. For a long while she carried a penknife in her handbag in case she should need to defend herself. One evening, after they had been out with a colleague of Graham's and had had a few drinks, she told Graham about this fear of hers.

He said she was silly but he seemed rather pleased.

'When you went off to talk to those people and I was left with John I felt like that. I felt terribly nervous. I didn't know how to talk to him.'

Graham roared with laughter. 'You don't mean you thought old John was going to make a pass at you in the middle of a crowded restaurant?'

'I don't know,' Christine said. 'I never know what they'll do.'

'So long as you're not afraid of what I'll do,' said Graham, beginning to kiss her, 'that's all that matters.'

There was no point in telling him now, ten years too late, that she was afraid of what he did and always had been. Of course she had got used to it, she wasn't actually terrified, she was resigned and sometimes even quite cheerful about it. David was the only man she had ever been alone with when it felt all right.

That first time, that Thursday when Angie had gone to her sister's and hadn't been able to get through on the phone and tell Christine not to come, that time it had been fine. And afterwards she had felt happy and carefree, though what had happened with David took on the colouring of a dream next day. It wasn't really believable. Early on he had said:

'Will you tell Angie?'

'Not if you don't want me to.

'I think it would upset her, Chris. It might even wreck our marriage. You see . . .' He had hesitated. 'You see, that was the first time I - I mean, anyone ever . . .' And he had looked into her eyes. Thank God it was you.'

The following Thursday she had gone round to see Angie as usual. In the meantime there had been no word from David. She stayed late in order to see him, beginning to feel a little sick with apprehension, her heart beating hard when he came in.

He looked quite different from how he had when she had found him sitting at the table reading, the radio on. He was wearing a grey flannel suit and a grey striped tie. When Angie went out of the room and for a minute she was alone with him, she felt a flicker of that old wariness that was the forerunner of her fear. He was getting her a drink. She looked up and met his eyes and it was all right again. He gave her a conspiratorial smile, laying a finger on his lips.

'I'll give you a ring,' he had whispered.

She had to wait two more weeks. During that time she went twice to Angie's and twice Angie came to her. She and Graham and Angie and David went out as a foursome and while Graham was fetching drinks and Angie was in the Ladies, David looked at her and smiled and lightly touched her foot with his foot under the table.

'I'll phone you. I haven't forgotten.'

It was a Wednesday when he finally did phone. Next day Christine told Graham she had made a new friend, a girl she had met at work. She would be going out somewhere with this new friend on Friday and she wouldn't be back till eleven. She was desperately afraid he would want the car - it was his car or his firm's - but it so happened he would be in the office that day and would go by train. Telling him these lies didn't make her feel guilty. It wasn't as if this were some sordid affair, it was quite different.

When Friday came she dressed with great care. Normally, to go round to Angie's, she would have worn jeans and a teeshirt with a sweater over it. That was what she had on the first time she found herself alone with David. She put on a skirt and blouse and her black velvet jacket. She took the heated rollers out of her hair and brushed it into curls down on her shoulders. There was never much money to spend on clothes. The mortgage on the house took up a third of what Graham earned and half what she earned at her part-time job. But she could run to a pair of sheer black tights to go with the highest-heeled shoes she'd got, her black pumps.

The doors of Angie and David's garage were wide open and their car was gone. Christine turned into their driveway, drove into the garage and closed the doors behind her. A door at the back of the garage led into the yard and garden. The kitchen door was unlocked as it had been that Thursday three weeks before and always was on Thursday afternoons. She opened the door and walked in.

'Is that you, Chris?'

The voice sounded very male. She needed to be reassured by the sight of him. She went into the hall as he came down the stairs.

'You look lovely,' he said.

'So do you.'

He was wearing a suit. It was of navy silk with a pattern of pink and white flowers. The skirt was very short, the jacket clinched into his waist with a wide navy patent belt. The long golden hair fell to his shoulders, he was heavily made-up and this time he had painted his fingernails. He looked far more beautiful than he had that first time.

Then, three weeks before, the sound of her entry drowned in loud music from the radio, she had come upon this girl sitting at the table reading Vogue. For a moment she had thought it must be David's sister. She had forgotten Angie had said David was an only child. The girl had long fair hair and was wearing a red summer dress with white spots on it, white sandals and around her neck a string of white beads. When Christine saw that it was not a girl but David himself she didn't know what to do.

He stared at her in silence and without moving and then he switched off the radio. Christine said the silliest and least relevant thing.

'What are you doing home at this time?'

That made him smile. 'I'd finished so I took the rest of the day off. I should have locked the back door. Now you're here you may as well sit down.'

She sat down. She couldn't take her eyes off him. He didn't look like a man dressed up as a girl, he looked like a girl and a much prettier one than she or Angie. 'Does Angie know?'

He shook his head.

'But why do you do it?' she burst out and she looked about the room, Angle's small, rather untidy living room, at the radio, the *Vogue* magazine. 'What do you get out of it?' Something came back to her from an article she had read. 'Did your mother dress you as a girl when you were little?'

'I don't know,' he said. 'Maybe. I don't remember. I don't want to be a girl. I just want to dress up as one sometimes.'

The first shock of it was past and she began to feel easier with him. It wasn't as if there was anything grotesque about the way he looked. The very last thing he reminded her of was one of those female impersonators. A curious thought came into her head, that it was *nicer,* somehow more civilised, to be a woman and that if only all men were more like women . . . That was silly, of course, it couldn't be.

'And it's enough for you just to dress up and be here on your own?'

He was silent for a moment. Then, 'Since you ask, what I'd really like would be to go out like this and . . .' He paused, looking at her, ' . . . and be seen by lots of people, that's what I'd like. I've never had the nerve for that.'

The bold idea expressed itself without her having to give it a moment's thought. She wanted to do it. She was beginning to tremble with excitement.

'Let's go out then, you and I. Let's go out now. I'll put my car in your garage and you can get into it so the people next door don't see and then we'll go somewhere. Let's do that, David, shall we?'

She wondered afterwards why she had enjoyed it so much. What had it been, after all, as far as anyone else knew but two girls walking on Hampstead Heath? If Angie had suggested that the two of them do it she would have thought it a poor way of spending the afternoon. But with David . . . She hadn't even minded that of the two of them he was infinitely the better dressed, taller, better-looking, more graceful. She didn't mind now as he came down the stairs and stood in front of her.

'Where shall we go?'

'Not the Heath this time,' he said. 'Let's go shopping.'

He bought a blouse in one of the big stores. Christine went

into the changing room with him when he tried it on. They walked about in Hyde Park. Later on they had dinner and Christine noted that they were the only two women in the restaurant dining together.

'I'm grateful to you,' David said. He put his hand over hers on the table.

'I enjoy it,' she said. 'It's so - crazy. I really love it. You'd better not do that, had you? There's a man over there giving a funny look.

'Women hold hands,' he said.

'Only those sort of women. David, we could do this every Friday you don't have to work.'

'Why not?' he said.

There was nothing to feel guilty about. She wasn't harming Angie and she wasn't being disloyal to Graham. All she was doing was going on innocent outings with another girl. Graham wasn't interested in her new friend, he didn't even ask her name. Christine came to long for Fridays, especially for the moment when she let herself into Angie's house and saw David coming down the stairs and for the moment when they stepped out of the car in some public place and the first eyes were turned on him. They went to Holland Park, they went to the zoo, to Kew Gardens. They went to the cinema and a man sitting next to David put his hand on his knee. David loved that, it was a triumph for him, but Christine whispered they must change their seats and they did.

When they parted at the end of an evening he kissed her gently on the lips. He smelt of *Alliage* or *Je Reviens* or Opium. During the afternoon they usually went into one of the big stores and sprayed themselves out of the tester bottles.

Angie's mother lived in the north of England. When she had to convalesce after an operation Angie went up there to look after her. She expected to be away two weeks and the second weekend of her absence Graham had to go to Brussels with the sales manager.

'We could go away somewhere for the weekend,' David said.

'Graham's sure to phone,' Christine said.

'One night then. lust for the Saturday night. You can tell him you're going out with your new girlfriend and you're going to be late.'

'All right.'

It worried her that she had no nice clothes to wear. David had a small but exquisite wardrobe of suits and dresses, shoes and scarves and beautiful underclothes. He kept them in a cupboard in his office to which only he had a key and he secreted items home and back again in his briefcase. Christine hated the idea of going away for the night in her grey flannel skirt and white silk blouse and that velvet jacket while David wore his Zandra Rhodes dress. In a burst of recklessness she spent all of two weeks' wages on a linen suit.

They went in David's car. He had made the arrangements and Christine had expected they would be going to a motel twenty miles outside London. She hadn't thought it would matter much to David where they went. But he surprised her by his choice of an hotel that was a three-hundred-year-old house on the Suffolk coast.

'If we're going to do it,' he said, 'we may as well do it in style.'

She felt very comfortable with him, very happy. She tried to imagine what it would have felt like going to spend a night in an hotel with a man, a lover. If the person sitting next to her were dressed, not in a black and white printed silk dress and scarlet jacket but in a man's suit with shirt and tie. If the face it gave her so much pleasure to look at were not powdered and rouged and mascara'd but rough and already showing beard growth. She couldn't imagine it. Or, rather, she could only think how in that case she would have jumped out of the car at the first red traffic lights.

They had single rooms next door to each other. The rooms were very small but Christine could see that a double might have been awkward for David who must at some point - though she didn't care to think of this - have to shave and strip down to being what he really was.

He came in and sat on her bed while she unpacked her nightdress and spare pair of shoes.

'This is fun, isn't it?'

She nodded, squinting into the mirror, working on her eyelids with a little brush. David always did his eyes beautifully. She turned round and smiled at him.

'Let's go down and have a drink.'

The dining room, the bar, the lounge were all low-ceilinged timbered rooms with carved wood on the walls David said was called linenfold panelling. There were old maps and pictures of men hunting in gilt frames and copper bowls full of roses. Long windows were thrown open on to a terrace. The sun was still high in the sky and it was very warm. While Christine sat on the terrace in the sunshine David went off to get their drinks. When he came back to their table he had a man with him, a thickset paunchy man of about forty who was carrying a tray with four glasses on it.

'This is Ted,' David said.

'Delighted to meet you,' Ted said. 'I've asked my friend to join us. I hope you don't mind.'

She had to say she didn't. David looked at her and from his look she could tell he had deliberately picked Ted up.

'But why did you?' she said to him afterwards. 'Why did you want to? You told me you didn't really like it when that man put his hand on you in the cinema.'

'That was so physical. This is just a laugh. You don't suppose I'd let them touch me, do you?'

Ted and Peter had the next table to theirs at dinner. Christine was silent and standoffish but David flirted with them. Ted kept leaning across and whispering to him and David giggled and smiled. You could see he was enjoying himself tremendously. Christine knew they would ask her and David to go out with them after dinner and she began to be afraid. Suppose David got carried away by the excitement of it, the 'fun', and went off somewhere with Ted, leaving her and Peter alone together? Peter had a red face and a black moustache and beard and a wart with black hairs growing out of it on his left cheek. She and David were eating steak and the waiter had brought them sharp pointed steak knives. She hadn't used hers. The steak was very tender. When no one was looking she slipped the steak knife into her bag.

Ted and Peter were still drinking coffee and brandies when David got up quite abruptly and said, 'Coming?' to Christine.

'I suppose you've arranged to meet them later?' Christine said as soon as they were out of the dining room.

David looked at her. His scarlet-painted lips parted into a wide smile. He laughed.

'I turned them down.'

'Did you really?'

'I could tell you hated the idea. Besides, we want to be atone, don't we? I know I want to be alone with you.'

She nearly shouted his name so that everyone could hear, the relief was so great. She controlled herself but she was trembling. 'Of course I want to be alone with you,' she said.

She put her arm in his. It wasn't uncommon, after all, for girls to walk along with linked arms. Men turned to look at David and one of them whistled. She knew it must be David the whistle was directed at because he looked so beautiful with his long golden hair and high-heeled red sandals. They walked along the sea front, along the little low promenade. It was too warm even at eight-thirty to wear a coat. There were a lot of people about but not crowds for the place was too select to attract crowds. They walked to the end of the pier. They had a drink in the Ship Inn and another in the Fishermen's Arms. A man tried to pick David up in the Fishermen's Arms but this time he was cold and distant.

'I'd like to put my arm round you,' he said as they were walking back, 'but I suppose that wouldn't do, though it is dark.'

'Better not,' said Christine. She said suddenly, 'This has been the best evening of my life.'

He looked at her. 'You really mean that?' She nodded. 'Absolutely the best.'

They came into the hotel. 'I'm going to get them to send us up a couple of drinks. To my room. Is that okay?'

She sat on the bed. David went into the bathroom. To do his face, she thought, maybe to shave before he let the man with the drinks see him. There was a knock at the door and a waiter came in with a tray on which were two long glasses of something or other with fruit and leaves floating in it, two pink table napkins, two olives on sticks and two peppermint creams wrapped up in green paper.

Christine tasted one of the drinks. She ate an olive. She opened her handbag and took out a mirror and a lipstick and painted her lips. David came out of the bathroom. He had taken off the golden wig and washed his face. He hadn't shaved, there was a pale stubble showing on his chin and cheeks. His legs and feet were bare and he was wearing a very masculine robe made of navy blue towelling. She tried to hide her disappointment.

'You've changed,' she said brightly.

He shrugged. 'There are limits.'

He raised his glass and she raised her glass and he said; 'To us!'

The beginnings of a feeling of panic came over her. Suddenly he was so evidently a man. She edged a little way along the mattress.

'I wish we had the whole weekend.'

She nodded nervously. She was aware her body had started a faint trembling. He had noticed it too. Sometimes before he had noticed how emotion made her tremble.

'Chris,' he said.

She sat passive and afraid.

'I'm not really like a woman, Chris. I just play at that sometimes for fun. You know that, don't you?' The hand that touched her smelt of nail varnish remover. There were hairs on the wrist she had never noticed before. 'I'm falling in love with you,' he said 'And you feel the same, don't you?'

She couldn't speak. He took her by the shoulders. He brought his mouth up to hers and put his arms round her and began kissing her. His skin felt abrasive and a smell as male as Graham's came off his body. She shook and shuddered. He pushed her down on the bed and his hands began undressing her, his mouth still on hers and his body heavy on top of her.

She felt behind her, put her hand into the open handbag and pulled out the knife. Because she could feel his heart beating steadily against her right breast she knew where to stab and she stabbed again and again. The bright red heart's blood spurted over her clothes and the bed and the two peppermint creams on the tray.

THE MACHINE STOPS

– E.M. FORSTER

***

PART ONE: THE AIR-SHIP

IMAGINE, if you can, a small room, hexagonal in shape, like the cell of a bee. It is lighted neither by window nor by lamp, yet it is filled with a soft radiance. There are no apertures for ventilation, yet the air is fresh. There are no musical instruments, and yet, at the moment that my meditation opens, this room is throbbing with melodious sounds. An armchair is in the centre, by its side a reading-desk - that is all the furniture. And in the armchair there sits a swaddled lump of flesh - a woman, about five feet high, with a face as white as a fungus. It is to her that the little room belongs.

An electric bell rang.

The woman touched a switch and the music was silent.

'I suppose I must see who it is,' she thought, and set her chair in motion. The chair, like the music, was worked by machinery, and it rolled her to the other side of the room, where the bell still rang importunately.

'Who is it?' she called. Her voice was irritable, for she had been interrupted often since the music began. She knew several thousand people; in certain directions human intercourse had advanced enormously.

But when she listened into the receiver, her white face wrinkled into smiles, and she said:

'Very well. Let us talk, I will isolate myself. I do not expect anything important will happen for the next five minutes - for I can give you fully five minutes, Kuno. Then I must deliver my lecture on "Music during the Australian Period"

She touched the isolation knob, so that no one else could speak to her. Then she touched the lighting apparatus, and the little room was plunged into darkness.

'Be quick!' she called, her irritation returning. 'Be quick, Kuno; here I am in the dark wasting my time.'

But it was fully fifteen seconds before the round plate that she held in her hands began to glow. A faint blue light shot across it, darkening to purple, and presently she could see the image of her son, who lived on the other side of the earth, and he could see her.

'Kuno, how slow you are.'

He smiled gravely.

'I really believe you enjoy dawdling.'

'I have called you before, mother, but you were always busy or isolated. I have something particular to say.'

'What is it, dearest boy? Be quick. Why could you not send it by pneumatic post?'

'Because I prefer saying such a thing. I want —'

'Well?'

'I want you to come and see me.'

Vashti watched his face in the blue plate.

'But I can see you!' she exclaimed. 'What more do you want?'

'I want to see you not through the Machine,' said Kuno. 'I want to speak to you not through the wearisome Machine.'

'Oh, hush!' said his mother, vaguely shocked. 'You mustn't say anything against the Machine.'

'Why not?'

'One mustn't.'

'You talk as if a god had made the Machine,' cried the other. 'I believe that you pray to it when you are unhappy. Men made it, do not forget that. Great men, but men. The Machine is much, but it is not everything. I see something like you in this plate, but I do not see you. I hear something like you through this telephone, but I do not hear you. That is why I want you to come. Come and stop with me. Pay me a visit, so that we can meet face to face, and talk about the hopes that are in my mind.'

She replied that she could scarcely spare the time for a visit.

'The airship barely takes two days to fly between me and you.'

'I dislike airships.'

'Why?'

'I dislike seeing the horrible brown earth, and the sea, and the stars when it is dark. I get no ideas in an airship.'

'I do not get them anywhere else.'

'What kind of ideas can the air give you?'

He paused for an instant.

'Do you not know four big stars that form an oblong, and three stars close together in the middle of the oblong, and hanging from these stars, three other stars?'

'No, I do not. I dislike the stars. But did they give you an idea? How interesting; tell me.'

'I had an idea that they were like a man.'

'I do not understand.'

'The four big stars are the man's shoulders and his knees. The three stars in the middle are like the belts that men wore once, and the three stars hanging are like a sword.'

'A sword?'

'Men carried swords about with them, to kill animals and other men.'

'It does not strike me as a very good idea, but it is certainly original. When did it come to you first?'

'In the airship —' He broke off, and she fancied that he looked sad. She could not be sure, for the Machine did not transmit *nuances* of expression. It only gave a general idea of people - an idea that was good enough for all practical purposes, Vashti thought. The imponderable bloom, declared by a discredited philosophy to be the actual essence of intercourse, was rightly ignored by the Machine, just as the imponderable bloom of the grape was ignored by the manufacturers of artificial fruit. Something 'good enough' had long since been accepted by our race.

'The truth is,' he continued, 'that I want to see these stars again. They are curious stars. I want to see them not from the airship, but from the surface of the earth, as our ancestors did, thousands of years ago. I want to visit the surface of the earth.' She was shocked again.

'Mother, you must come, if only to explain to me what is the harm of visiting the surface of the earth.'

'No harm,' she replied, controlling herself. 'But no advantage. The surface of the earth is only dust and mud, no life remains on it, and you would need a respirator, or the cold of the outer air would kill you. One dies immediately in the outer air.'

'I know; of course I shall take all precautions.'

'And besides —'

'Well?'

She considered, and chose her words with care. Her son had a queer temper, and she wished to dissuade him from the expedition.

'It is contrary to the spirit of the age,' she asserted.

'Do you mean by that, contrary to the Machine?'

'In a sense, but —'

His image in the blue plate faded.

'Kuno!'

He had isolated himself.

For a moment Vashti felt lonely.

Then she generated the light, and the sight of her room, flooded with radiance and studded with electric buttons, revived her. There were buttons and switches everywhere - buttons to call for food, for music, for clothing. There was the hot-bath button, by pressure of which a basin of (imitation) marble rose out of the floor, filled to the brim with a warm deodorized liquid. There was the cold-bath button. There was the button that produced literature. And there were of course the buttons by which she communicated with her friends. The room, though it contained nothing, was in touch with all that she cared for in the world.

Vashti's next move was to turn off the isolation-switch, and all the accumulations of the last three minutes burst upon her. The room was filled with the noise of bells, and speaking-tubes. What was the new food like? Could she recommend it? Had she had any ideas lately? Might one tell her one's own ideas? Would she make an engagement to visit the public nurseries at an early date? - say this day month.

To most of these questions she replied with irritation - a growing quality in that accelerated age. She said that the new food was horrible. That she could not visit the public nurseries through press of engagements. That she had no ideas of her own but had just been told one - that four stars and three in the middle were like a man:

she doubted there was much in it. Then she switched off her correspondents, for it was time to deliver her lecture on Australian music.

The clumsy system of public gatherings had been long since abandoned; neither Vashti nor her audience stirred from their rooms. Seated in her armchair she spoke, while they in their armchairs heard her, fairly well, and saw her, fairly well. She opened with a humorous account of music in the pre-

Mongolian epoch, and went on to describe the great outburst of song that followed the Chinese conquest. Remote and primaeval as were the methods of I-San-So and the Brisbane school, she yet felt (she said) that study of them might repay the musician of today: they had freshness; they had, above all, ideas.

Her lecture, which lasted ten minutes, was well received, and at its conclusion, she and many of her audience listened to a lecture on the sea; there were ideas to be got from the sea; the speaker had donned a respirator and visited it lately. Then she fed, talked to many friends, had a bath, talked again, and summoned her bed.

The bed was not to her liking. It was too large, and she had a feeling for a small bed. Complaint was useless, for beds were of the same dimension all over the world, and to have had an alternative size would have involved vast alterations in the Machine. Vashti isolated herself - it was necessary, for neither day nor night existed under the ground - and reviewed all that had happened since she had summoned the bed last. Ideas? Scarcely any. Events - was Kuno's invitation an event?

By her side, on the little reading-desk, was a survival from the ages of litter - one book. This was the Book of the Machine. In it were instructions against every possible contingency. If she was hot or cold or dyspeptic or at a loss for a word, she went to the book, and it told her which button to press. The Central Committee published it. In accordance with a growing habit, it was richly bound.

Sitting up in the bed, she took it reverently in her hands. She glanced round the glowing room as if some one might be watching her. Then, half ashamed, half joyful, she murmured 'O Machine! 0 Machine!' and raised the volume to her lips. Thrice she kissed it, thrice inclined her head, thrice she felt the delirium of acquiescence. Her ritual performed, she turned to page 1367, which gave the times of the departure of the airships from the island in the southern hemisphere, under whose soil she lived, to the island in the northern hemisphere, whereunder lived her son.

She thought, 'I have not the time.'

She made the room dark and slept; she awoke and made the room light; she ate and exchanged ideas with her friends, and listened to music and attended lectures; she made the room dark and slept. Above her, beneath her, and around her, the Machine hummed eternally; she did not notice the noise, for she had been born with it in her ears. The earth, carrying her, hummed as it sped through silence, turning her now to the invisible sun, now to the invisible stars. She awoke and made the room light.

'Kuno!'

'I will not talk to you,' he answered, 'until you come.'

'Have you been on the surface of the earth since we spoke last?'

His image faded.

Again she consulted the book. She became very nervous and lay back in her chair palpitating. Think of her as without teeth or hair. Presently she directed the chair to the wall, and pressed an unfamiliar button. The wall swung apart slowly. Through the opening she saw a tunnel that curved slightly, so that its goal was not visible. Should she go to see her son, here was the beginning of the journey.

Of course she knew all about the communication-system. There was nothing mysterious in it. She would summon a car and it would fly with her down the tunnel until it reached the lift that communicated with the airship station: the system had been in use for many, many years, long before the universal establishment of the Machine. And of course she had studied the civilization that had immediately preceded her own - the civilization that had mistaken the functions of the system, and had used it for bringing people to things, instead of for bringing things to people. Those funny old days, when men went for change of air instead of changing the air in their rooms! And yet - she was frightened of the tunnel: she had not seen it since her last child was born. It curved - but not quite as she remembered; it was brilliant - but not quite as brilliant as a lecturer had suggested. Vashti was seized with the terrors of direct experience. She shrank back into the room, and the wall closed up again.

'Kuno,' she said, 'I cannot come to see you. I am not well.'

Immediately an enormous apparatus fell on to her out of the ceiling, a thermometer was automatically inserted between her lips, a stethoscope was automatically laid upon her heart. She lay powerless. Cool pads soothed her forehead. Kuno had telegraphed to her doctor.

So the human passions still blundered up and down in the Machine. Vashti drank the medicine that the doctor projected into her mouth, and the machinery retired into the ceiling. The voice of Kuno was heard asking how she felt.

'Better.' Then with irritation: 'But why do you not come to me instead?'

'Because I cannot leave this place.'

'Why?'

'Because, any moment, something tremendous may happen.'

'Have you been on the surface of the earth yet?'

'Not yet.'

'Then what is it?'

'I will not tell you through the Machine.'

She resumed her life.

But she thought of Kuno as a baby, his birth, his removal to the public nurseries, her one visit to him there, his visits to her - visits which stopped when the Machine had assigned him a room on the other side of the earth. 'Parents, duties of,' said the book of the Machine, 'cease at the moment of birth. P. 422327483.' True, but there was something special about Kuno - indeed there had been something special about all her children - and, after all, she must brave the journey if he desired it. And 'something tremendous might happen.' What did that mean? The nonsense of a youthful man, no doubt, but she must go. Again she pressed the unfamiliar button, again the wall swung back, and she saw the tunnel that curved out of sight. Clasping the Book, she rose, tottered on to the platform, and summoned the car. Her room closed behind her: the journey to the northern hemisphere had begun.

Of course it was perfectly easy. The car approached and in it she found armchairs exactly like her own. When she signalled, it stopped, and she tottered into the lift. One other passenger was in the lift, the first fellow creature she had seen face to face for months. Few travelled in these days, for, thanks to the advance of science, the earth was exactly alike all over. Rapid intercourse, from which the previous civilization had hoped so much, had ended by defeating itself. What was the good of going to Pekin when it was just like Shrewsbury? Why return to Shrewsbury when it would be just like Pekin? Men seldom moved their bodies; all unrest was concentrated in the soul.

The airship service was a relic from the former age. It was kept up, because it was easier to keep it up than to stop it or to diminish it, but it now far exceeded the wants of the population. Vessel after vessel would rise from the vomitories of Rye or of Christchurch (I use the antique names), would sail into the crowded sky, and would draw up at the wharves of the south - empty. So nicely adjusted was the system, so independent of meteorology, that the sky, whether calm or cloudy, resembled a vast kaleidoscope whereon the same patterns periodically recurred. The ship on which Vashti sailed started now at sunset, now at dawn. But always, as it passed above Rheims, it would neighbour the ship that served between Helsingfors and the Brazils, and, every third time it surmounted the Alps, the fleet of Palermo would cross its track behind. Night and day, wind and storm, tide and earthquake, impeded man no longer. He had harnessed Leviathan. All the old literature, with its praise of Nature, and its fear of Nature, rang false as the prattle of a child.

Yet as Vashti saw the vast flank of the ship, stained with exposure to the outer air, her horror of direct experience returned. It was not quite like the airship in the cinematophote. For one thing it smelt -not strongly or unpleasantly, but it did smell, and with her eyes shut she should have known that a new thing was close to her. Then she had to walk to it from the lift, had to submit to glances from the other passengers. The man in front dropped his Book - no great matter, but it disquieted them all. In the rooms, if the Book was dropped, the floor raised it mechanically, but the gangway to the airship was not so prepared, and the sacred volume lay motionless. They stopped - the thing was unforeseen - and the man, instead of picking up his property, felt the muscles of his arm to see how they had failed him. Then some one actually said with direct utterance: 'We shall be late' - and they trooped on board, Vashti treading on the pages as she did so.

Inside, her anxiety increased. The arrangements were old-fashioned and rough. There was even a female attendant, to whom she would have to announce her wants during the voyage. Of course a revolving platform ran the length of the boat, but she was expected to walk from it to her cabin. Some cabins were better than others, and she did not get the best. She thought the attendant had been unfair, and spasms of rage shook her. The glass valves had closed, she could not go back. She saw, at the end of the vestibule, the lift in which she had ascended going quietly up and down, empty. Beneath those corridors of shining tiles were rooms, tier below tier, reaching far into the earth, and in each room there sat a human being, eating, or sleeping, or producing ideas. And buried deep in the hive was her own room. Vashti was afraid.

'O Machine! O Machine!' she murmured, and caressed her Book, and was comforted.

Then the sides of the vestibule seemed to melt together, as do the passages that we see in dreams, the lift vanished, the Book that had been dropped slid to the left and vanished, polished tiles rushed by like a stream of water, there was a slight jar, and the airship, issuing from its tunnel, soared above the waters of a tropical ocean.

It was night. For a moment she saw the coast of Sumatra edged by the phosphorescence of waves, and crowned by lighthouses, still sending forth their disregarded beams. These also vanished, and only the stars distracted her. They were not motionless, but swayed to and fro above her head, thronging out of one skylight into another, as if the universe and not the airship was careening. And, as often happens on clear nights, they seemed now to be in perspective, now on a plane; now piled tier beyond tier into the infinite heavens, now concealing infinity, a roof limiting for ever the visions of men. In either case they seemed intolerable. 'Are we to travel in the dark?' called the passengers angrily, and the attendant, who had been careless, generated the light, and pulled down the blinds of pliable metal. When the airships had been built, the desire to look direct at things still lingered in the world. Hence the extraordinary number of skylights and windows, and the proportionate discomfort to those who were civilized and refined. Even in Vashti's cabin one star peeped through a flaw in the blind, and after a few hours' uneasy slumber, she was disturbed by an unfamiliar glow, which was the dawn.

Quick as the ship had sped westwards, the earth had rolled eastwards quicker still, and had dragged back Vashti and her companions towards the sun. Science could prolong the night, but only for a little, and those high hopes of neutralizing the earth's diurnal revolution had passed, together with hopes that were possibly higher. To 'keep pace with the sun,' or even to outstrip it, had been the aim of the civilization preceding this. Racing aeroplanes had been built for the purpose, capable of enormous speed, and steered by the greatest intellects of the epoch. Round the globe they went, round and round, westward, westward, round and round, amidst humanity's applause. In vain. The globe went eastward quicker still, horrible accidents occurred, and the Committee of the Machine, at the time rising into prominence, declared the pursuit illegal, unmechanical, and punishable by Homelessness.

Of Homelessness more will be said later.

Doubtless the Committee was right. Yet the attempt to 'defeat the sun' aroused the last common interest that our race experienced about the heavenly bodies, or indeed about anything. It was the last time that men were compacted by thinking of a power outside the world. The sun had conquered, yet it was the end of his spiritual dominion. Dawn, midday, twilight, the zodiacal path, touched neither men's lives nor their hearts, and science retreated into the ground, to concentrate herself upon problems that she was certain of solving.

So when Vashti found her cabin invaded by a rosy finger of light, she was annoyed, and tried to adjust the blind. But the blind flew up altogether, and she saw through the skylight small pink clouds, swaying against a background of blue, and as the sun crept higher, its radiance entered direct, brimming down the wall, like a golden sea. It rose and fell with the airship's motion, just as waves rise and fall, but it advanced steadily, as a tide advances. Unless she was careful, it would strike her face. A spasm of horror shook her and she rang for the attendant. The attendant too was horrified, but she could do nothing; it was not her place to mend the blind. She could only suggest that the lady should change her cabin, which she accordingly prepared to do.

People were almost exactly alike all over the world, but the attendant of the airship, perhaps owing to her exceptional duties, had grown a little out of the common. She had often to address passengers with direct speech, and this had given her a certain roughness and originality of manner. When Vashti swerved away from the sunbeams with a cry, she behaved barbarically - she put out her hand to steady her.

'How dare you!' exclaimed the passenger. 'You forget yourself!'

The woman was confused, and apologized for not having let her fall. People never touched one another. The custom had become obsolete, owing to the Machine.

'Where are we now?' asked Vashti haughtily.

'We are over Asia,' said the attendant, anxious to be polite.

'Asia?'

'You must excuse my common way of speaking. I have got into the habit of calling places over which I pass by their unmechanical names.'

'Oh, I remember Asia. The Mongols came from it.'

'Beneath us, in the open air, stood a city that was once called Simla.'

'Have you ever heard of the Mongols and of the Brisbane school?'

'No.'

'Brisbane also stood in the open air.'

'Those mountains to the right - let me show you them.' She pushed back a metal blind. The main chain of the Himalayas was revealed. 'They were once called the Roof of the World, those mountains.'

'What a foolish name!'

'You must remember that, before the dawn of civilization, they seemed to be an impenetrable wall that touched the stars. It was supposed that no one but the gods could exist above their summits. How we have advanced, thanks to the Machine!'

'How we have advanced, thanks to the Machine!' said Vashti.

'How we have advanced, thanks to the Machine!' echoed the passenger who had dropped his Book the night before, and who was standing in the passage.

'And that white stuff in the cracks? - what is it?'

'I have forgotten its name.'

'Cover the window, please. These mountains give me no ideas.'

The northern aspect of the Himalayas was in deep shadow: on the Indian slope the sun had just prevailed. The forests had been destroyed during the literature epoch for the purpose of making newspaper-pulp, but the snows were awakening to their morning glory, and clouds still hung on the breasts of Kinchinjunga. In the plain were seen the ruins of cities, with diminished rivers creeping by their walls, and by the sides of these were sometimes the signs of vomitories, marking the cities of today. Over the whole prospect airships rushed, crossing and intercrossing with incredible *aplomb*, and rising nonchalantly when they desired to escape the perturbations of the lower atmosphere and to traverse the Roof of the World.

'We have indeed advanced, thanks to the Machine,' repeated the attendant, and hid the Himalayas behind a metal blind.

The day dragged wearily forward. The passengers sat each

in his cabin, avoiding one another with an almost physical repulsion and longing to be once more under the surface of the earth. There were eight or ten of them, mostly young males, sent out from the public nurseries to inhabit the rooms of those who had died in various parts of the earth. The man who had dropped his Book was on the homeward journey. He had been sent to Sumatra for the purpose of propagating the race. Vashti alone was travelling by her private will.

At midday she took a second glance at the earth. The airship was crossing another range of mountains, but she could see little, owing to clouds. Masses of black rock hovered below her, and merged indistinctly into grey. Their shapes were fantastic; one of them resembled a prostrate man.

'No ideas here,' murmured Vashti, and hid the Caucasus behind a metal blind.

In the evening she looked again. They were crossing a golden sea, in which lay many small islands and one peninsula.

She repeated, 'No ideas here,' and hid Greece behind a metal blind.

PART TWO: THE MENDING APPARATUS

By a vestibule, by a lift, by a tubular railway, by a platform, by a sliding door - by reversing all the steps of her departure did Vashti arrive at her son's room, which exactly resembled her own. She might well declare that the visit was superfluous. The buttons, the knobs, the reading-desk with the Book, the temperature, the atmosphere, the illumination - all were exactly the same. And if Kuno himself, flesh of her flesh, stood close beside her at last, what profit was there in that? She was too well-bred to shake him by the hand.

Averting her eyes, she spoke as follows:

'Here I am. I have had the most terrible journey and greatly retarded the development of my soul. It is not worth it, Kuno, it is not worth it. My time is too precious. The sunlight almost touched me, and I have met with the rudest people. I can only stop a few minutes. Say what you want to say, and then I must return.'

'I have been threatened with Homelessness,' said Kuno.

She looked at him now.

'I have been threatened with Homelessness, and I could not tell you such a thing through the Machine.'

Homelessness means death. The victim is exposed to the air, which kills him.

'I have been outside since I spoke to you last. The tremendous thing has happened, and they have discovered me.'

'But why shouldn't you go outside?' she exclaimed. 'It is perfectly legal, perfectly mechanical, to visit the surface of the earth. I have lately been to a lecture on the sea; there is no objection to that; one simply summons a respirator and gets an Egression-permit. It is not the kind of thing that spiritually-minded people do, and I begged you not to do it, but there is no legal objection to it.'

'I did not get an Egression-permit.'

'Then how did you get out?'

'I found out a way of my own.'

The phrase conveyed no meaning to her, and he had to repeat it.

'A way of your own?' she whispered. 'But that would be wrong.'

'Why?'

The question shocked her beyond measure.

'You are beginning to worship the Machine,' he said coldly. 'You think it irreligious of me to have found out a way of my own. It was just what the Committee thought, when they threatened me with Homelessness.'

At this she grew angry. 'I worship nothing!' she cried. 'I am most advanced. I don't think you irreligious, for there is no such thing as religion left. All the fear and the superstition that existed once have been destroyed by the Machine. I only meant that to find out a way of your own was – Besides, there is no new way out.'

'So it is always supposed.'

'Except through the vomitories, for which one must have an Egression-permit, it is impossible to get out. The Book says so.'

'Well, the Book's wrong, for I have been out on my feet.'

For Kuno was possessed of a certain physical strength.

By these days it was a demerit to be muscular. Each infant was examined at birth, and all who promised undue strength were destroyed. Humanitarians may protest, but it would have been no true kindness to let an athlete live; he would never have been happy in that state of life to which the Machine had called him; he would have yearned for trees to climb, rivers to bathe in, meadows and hills against which he might measure his body. Man must be adapted to his surroundings, must he not? In the dawn of the world our weakly must be exposed on Mount Taygetus, in its twilight our strong will suffer euthanasia, that the Machine may progress, that the Machine may progress, that the Machine may progress eternally.

'You know that we have lost the sense of space. We say "space is annihilated," but we have annihilated not space, but the sense thereof. We have lost a part of ourselves. I determined to recover it, and I began by walking up and down the platform of the railway outside my room. Up and down, until I was tired, and so did recapture the meaning of "Near" and "Far". "Near" is a place to which I can get quickly on my *feet,* not a place to which the train or the airship will take me quickly. "Far" is a place to which I cannot get quickly on my feet; the vomitory is "far," though I could be there in thirty-eight seconds by summoning the train. Man is the measure. That was my first lesson. Man's feet are the measure for distance, his hands are the measure for ownership, his body is the measure for all that is lovable and desirable and strong. Then I went further: it was then that I called to you for the first time, and you would not come.

This city, as you know, is built deep beneath the surface of the earth, with only the vomitories protruding. Having paced the platform outside my own room, I took the lift to the next platform and paced that also, and so with each in turn, until I came to the topmost, above which begins the earth. All the platforms were exactly alike, and all that I gained by visiting them was to develop my sense of space and my muscles. I think I should have been content with this - it is not a little thing, - but as I walked and brooded, it occurred to me that our cities had been built in the days when men still breathed the outer air, and that there had been ventilation shafts for the workmen. I could think of nothing but these ventilation shafts. Had they been destroyed by all the food-tubes and medicine-tubes and music-tubes that the Machine has evolved lately? Or did traces of them remain? One thing was certain. If I came upon them anywhere, it would be in the railway-tunnels of the topmost story. Everywhere else, all space was accounted for.

'I am telling my story quickly, but don't think that I was not a coward or that your answers never depressed me. It is not the proper thing, it is not mechanical, it is not decent to walk along a railway-tunnel. I did not fear that I might tread upon a live rail and be killed. I feared something far more intangible - doing what was not contemplated by the Machine. Then I said to myself, "Man is the measure," and I went, and after many visits I found an opening.

'The tunnels, of course, were lighted. Everything is light, artificial light; darkness is the exception. So when I saw a black gap in the tiles, I knew that it was an exception, and rejoiced. I put in my arm - I could put in no more at first - and waved it round and round in ecstasy. I loosened another tile, and put in my head, and shouted into the darkness: "I am coming, I shall do it yet," and my voice reverberated down endless passages. I seemed to hear the spirits of those dead workmen who had returned each evening to the starlight and to their wives, and all the generations who had lived in the open air called back to me, "You will do it yet, you are coming.'"

He paused, and, absurd as he was, his last words moved her. For Kuno had lately asked to be a father, and his request had been refused by the Committee. His was not a type that the Machine desired to hand on.

Then a train passed. It brushed by me, but I thrust my head and arms into the hole. I had done enough for one day, so I crawled back to the platform, went down in the lift, and summoned my bed. Ah what dreams! And again I called you, and again you refused.'

She shook her head and said:

'Don't. Don't talk of these terrible things. You make me miserable. You are throwing civilization away.'

'But I had got back the sense of space and a man cannot rest then. I determined to get in at the hole and climb the shaft. And so I exercised my arms. Day after day I went through ridiculous movements, until my flesh ached, and I could hang by my hands and hold the pillow of my bed outstretched for many minutes. Then I summoned a respirator, and started.

'It was easy at first. The mortar had somehow rotted, and I soon pushed some more tiles in, and clambered after them into the darkness, and the spirits of the dead comforted me. I don't know what I mean by that. I just say what I felt. I felt, for the first time, that a protest had been lodged against corruption, and that even as the dead were comforting me, so I was comforting the unborn. I felt that humanity existed, and that it existed without clothes. How can I possibly explain this? It was naked, humanity seemed naked, and all these tubes and buttons and machineries neither came into the world with us, nor will they follow us out, nor do they matter supremely while we are here. Had I been strong, I would have torn off every garment I had, and gone out into the outer air unswaddled. But this is not for me, nor perhaps for my generation. I climbed with my respirator and my hygienic clothes and my dietetic tabloids! Better thus than not at all.

'There was a ladder, made of some primaeval metal. The light from the railway fell upon its lowest rungs, and I saw that it led straight upwards out of the rubble at the bottom of the shaft. Perhaps our ancestors ran up and down it a dozen times daily, in their building. As I climbed, the rough edges cut through my gloves so that my hands bled. The light helped me for a little, and then came darkness and, worse still, silence which pierced my ears like a sword. The Machine hums! Did you know that? Its hum penetrates our blood, and may even guide our thoughts. Who knows? I was getting beyond its power. Then I thought: "This silence means that I am doing wrong." But I heard voices in the silence, and again they strengthened me.' He laughed. 'I had need of them. The next moment I cracked my head against something.'

She sighed.

'I had reached one of those pneumatic stoppers that defend us from the outer air. You may have noticed them on the airship. Pitch dark, my feet on the rungs of an invisible ladder, my hands cut; I cannot explain how I lived through this part, but the voices still comforted me, and I felt for fastenings. The stopper, I suppose, was about eight feet across. I passed my hand over it as far as I could reach. It was perfectly smooth. I felt it almost to the centre. Not quite to the centre, for my arm was too short. Then the voice said: "Jump. It is worth it. There may be a handle in the centre, and you may catch hold of it and so come to us your own way. And if there is no handle, so that you may fall and are dashed to pieces - it is still worth it: you will still come to us your own way." So I jumped. There was a handle, and —'

He paused. Tears gathered in his mother's eyes. She knew that he was fated. If he did not die today he would die tomorrow. There was not room for such a person in the world. And with her pity disgust mingled. She was ashamed at having borne such a son, she who had always been so respectable and so full of ideas. Was he really the little boy to whom she had taught the use of his stops and buttons, and to whom she had given his first lessons in the Book? The very hair that disfigured his lip showed that he was reverting to some savage type. On atavism the Machine can have no mercy.

'There was a handle, and I did catch it. I hung tranced over the darkness and heard the hum of these workings as the last whisper in a dying dream. All the things I had cared about and all the people I had spoken to through tubes appeared infinitely little. Meanwhile the handle revolved. My weight had set something in motion and I span slowly, and then –

'I cannot describe it. I was lying with my face to the sunshine. Blood poured from my nose and ears and I heard a tremendous roaring. The stopper, with me clinging to it, had simply been blown out of the earth, and the air that we make down here was escaping through the vent into the air above. It burst up like a fountain. 1 crawled back to it - for the upper air hurts - and, as it were, I took great sips from the edge. My respirator had flown goodness knows where, my clothes were torn. I just lay with my lips close to the hole, and I sipped until the bleeding stopped. You can imagine nothing so curious. This hollow in the grass - I will speak of it in a minute, - the sun shining into it, not brilliantly but through marbled clouds, - the peace, the nonchalance, the sense of space, and, brushing my cheek, the roaring fountain of our artificial air! Soon I spied my respirator, bobbing up and down in the current high above my head, and higher still were many airships. But no one ever looks out of airships, and in any case they could not have picked me up. There I was, stranded. The sun shone a little way down the shaft, and revealed the topmost rung of the ladder, but it was hopeless trying to reach it. I should either have been tossed up again by the escape, or else have fallen in, and died. I could only lie on the grass, sipping and sipping, and from time to time glancing around me.

'I knew that I was in Wessex, for I had taken care to go to a lecture on the subject before starting. Wessex lies above the room in which we are talking now. It was once an important state. Its kings held all the southern coast from the Andredswald to Cornwall, while the Wansdyke protected them on the north, running over the high ground. The lecturer was only concerned with the rise of Wessex, so I do not know how long it remained an international power, nor would the knowledge have assisted me. To tell the truth I could do nothing but laugh, during this part. There was I, with a pneumatic stopper by my side and a respirator bobbing over my head, imprisoned, all three of us, in a grass-grown hollow that was edged with fern.'

Then he grew grave again.

'Lucky for me that it was a hollow. For the air began to fall back into it and to fill it as water fills a bowl. I could crawl about. Presently I stood. I breathed a mixture, in which the air that hurts predominated whenever I tried to climb the sides. This was not so bad. I had not lost my tabloids and remained ridiculously cheerful, and as for the Machine, I forgot about it altogether. My one aim now was to get to the top, where the ferns were, and to view whatever objects lay beyond.

'I rushed the slope. The new air was still too bitter for me and I came rolling back, after a momentary vision of something grey. The sun grew very feeble, and I remembered that he was in Scorpio - I had been to a lecture on that too. If the sun is in Scorpio, and you are in Wessex, it means that you must be as quick as you can, or it will get too dark. (This is the first bit of useful information I have ever got from a lecture, and I expect it will be the last.) It made me try frantically to breathe the new air, and to advance as far as I dared out of my pond. The hollow filled so slowly. At times I thought that the fountain played with less vigour. My respirator seemed to dance nearer the earth; the roar was decreasing.'

He broke off.

'I don't think this is interesting you. The rest will interest you even less. There are no ideas in it, and I wish that I had not troubled you to come. We are too different, mother.'

She told him to continue.

'It was evening before I climbed the bank. The sun had very nearly slipped out of the sky by this time, and I could not get a good view. You, who have just crossed the Roof of the World, will not want to hear an account of the little hills that I saw - low colourless hills. But to me they were living and the turf that covered them was a skin, under which their muscles rippled, and I felt that those hills had called with incalculable force to men in the past, and that men had loved them. Now they sleep - perhaps for ever. They commune with humanity in dreams. Happy the man, happy the woman, who awakes the hills of Wessex. For though they sleep, they will never die.'

His voice rose passionately.

'Cannot you see, cannot all you lecturers see, that it is we that are dying, and that down here the only thing that really lives is the Machine? We created the Machine, to do our will, but we cannot make it do our will now. It has robbed us of the sense of space and of the sense of touch, it has blurred every human relation and narrowed down love to a carnal act, it has paralysed our bodies and our wills, and now it compels us to worship it. The Machine develops - but not on our lines. The Machine proceeds - but not to our goal. We only exist as the blood corpuscles that course through its arteries, and if it could work without us, it would let us die. Oh, I have no remedy - or, at least, only one - to tell men again and again that I have seen the hills of Wessex as Ælfrid saw them when he overthrew the Danes.

'So the sun set. I forgot to mention that a belt of mist lay between my hill and other hills, and that it was the colour of pearl.'

He broke off for the second time.

'Go on,' said his mother wearily.

He shook his head.

'Go on. Nothing that you say can distress me now. I am hardened.'

'I had meant to tell you the rest, but I cannot: I know that I cannot: goodbye.'

Vashti stood irresolute. All her nerves were tingling with his blasphemies. But she was also inquisitive.

'This is unfair,' she complained. 'You have called me across the world to hear your story, and hear it I will. Tell me - as briefly as possible, for this is a disastrous waste of time - tell me how you returned to civilization.'

'Oh - that!' he said, starting. 'You would like to hear about civilization. Certainly. Had I got to where my respirator fell down?'

'No - but I understand everything now. You put on your respirator, and managed to walk along the surface of the earth to a vomitory, and there your conduct was reported to the Central Committee.'

'By no means.'

He passed his hand over his forehead, as if dispelling some strong impression. Then, resuming his narrative, he warmed to it again.

'My respirator fell about sunset. I had mentioned that the fountain seemed feebler, had I not?'

'Yes.'

'About sunset, it let the respirator fall. As I said, I had entirely forgotten about the Machine, and I paid no great attention at the time, being occupied with other things. I had my pool of air, into which I could dip when the outer keenness became intolerable, and which would possibly remain for days, provided that no wind sprang up to disperse it. Not until it was too late did I realize what the stoppage of the escape implied. You see - the gap in the tunnel had been mended; the Mending Apparatus; the Mending Apparatus, was after me.

'One other warning I had, but I neglected it. The sky at night was clearer than it had been in the day, and the moon, which was about half the sky behind the sun, shone into the dell at moments quite brightly. I was in my usual place - on the boundary between the two atmospheres - when I thought I saw something dark move across the bottom of the dell, and vanish into the shaft. In my folly, I ran down. I bent over and listened, and I thought I heard a faint scraping noise in the depths.

'At this - but it was too late - I took alarm. I determined to put on my respirator and to walk right out of the dell. But my respirator had gone. I knew exactly where it had fallen - between the stopper and the aperture - and I could even feel the mark that it had made in the turf. It had gone, and I realized that something evil was at work, and I had better escape to the other air, and, if I must die, die running towards the cloud that had been the colour of a pearl. I never started. Out of the shaft - it is too horrible. A worm, a long white worm, had crawled out of the shaft and was gliding over the moonlit grass.

'I screamed. I did everything that I should not have done, I stamped upon the creature instead of flying from it, and it at once curled round the ankle. Then we fought. The worm let me run all over the dell, but edged up my leg as I ran. "Help!" I cried. (That part is too awful. It belongs to the part that you will never know.) "Help!" I cried. (Why cannot we suffer in silence?) "Help!" I cried. Then my feet were wound together, I fell, I was dragged away from the dear ferns and the living hills, and past the great metal stopper (I can tell you this part), and I thought it might save me again if I caught hold of the handle. It also was enwrapped, it also. Oh, the whole dell was full of the things. They were searching it in all directions, they were denuding it, and the white snouts of others peeped out of the hole, ready if needed. Everything that could be moved they brought -brushwood, bundles of fern, everything, and down we all went intertwined into hell. The last things that I saw, ere the stopper closed after us, were certain stars, and I felt that a man of my sort lived in the sky. For I did fight, I fought till the very end, and it was only my head hitting against the ladder that quieted me. I woke up in this room. The worms had vanished. I was surrounded by artificial air, artificial light, artificial peace, and my friends were calling to me down speaking-tubes to know whether I had come across any new ideas lately.'

Here his story ended. Discussion of it was impossible, and Vashti turned to go.

'It will end in Homelessness,' she said quietly.

'I wish it would,' retorted Kuno.

'The Machine has been most merciful.'

'I prefer the mercy of God.'

'By that superstitious phrase, do you mean that you could live in the outer air?'

'Yes.'

'Have you ever seen, round the vomitories, the bones of those who were extruded after the Great Rebellion?'

'Yes.'

They were left where they perished for our edification. A few crawled away, but they perished, too - who can doubt it? And so with the Homeless of our own day. The surface of the earth supports life no longer.'

'Indeed.'

'Ferns and a little grass may survive, but all higher forms have perished. Has any airship detected them?'

'No.'

'Has any lecturer dealt with them?'

'No.'

'Then why this obstinacy?'

'Because I have seen them,' he exploded.

'Seen what?'

'Because I have seen her in the twilight - because she came to my help when I called - because she, too, was entangled by the worms, and, luckier than I, was killed by one of them piercing her throat.'

He was mad. Vashti departed, nor, in the troubles that followed, did she ever see his face again.

PART THREE: THE HOMELESS

During the years that followed Kuno's escapade, two important developments took place in the Machine. On the surface they were revolutionary, but in either case men's minds had been prepared beforehand, and they did but express tendencies that were latent already.

The first of these was the abolition of respirators.

Advanced thinkers, like Vashti, had always held it foolish to visit the surface of the earth. Airships might be necessary, but what was the good of going out for mere curiosity and crawling along for a mile or two in a terrestrial motor? The habit was vulgar and perhaps faintly improper: it was unproductive of ideas, and had no connection with the habits that really mattered. So respirators were abolished, and with them, of course, the terrestrial motors, and except for a few lecturers, who complained that they were debarred access to their subject-matter, the development was accepted quietly. Those who still wanted to know what the earth was like had after all only to listen to some gramophone, or to look into some cinematophote. And even the lecturers acquiesced when they found that a lecture on the sea was none the less stimulating when compiled out of other lectures that had already been delivered on the same subject. 'Beware of firsthand ideas!' exclaimed one of the most advanced of them. 'First-hand ideas do not really exist. They are but the physical impressions produced by love and fear, and on this gross foundation who could erect a philosophy? Let your ideas be second-hand, and if possible tenth-hand, for then they will be far removed from that disturbing element - direct observation. Do not learn anything about this subject of mine - the French Revolution. Learn instead what I think that Enicharmon thought Urizen thought Gutch thought Ho-Yung thought Chi-Bo-Sing thought Lafcadio Hearn thought Carlyle thought Mirabeau said about the French Revolution. Through the medium of these ten great minds, the blood that was shed at Paris and the windows that were broken at Versailles will be clarified to an idea which you may employ most profitably in your daily lives. But be sure that the intermediates are many and varied, for in history one authority exists to counteract another. Urizen must counteract the scepticism of Ho-Yung and Enicharmon, I must myself counteract the impetuosity of

Gutch. You who listen to me are in a better position to judge about the French Revolution than I am. Your descendants will be even in a better position than you, for they will learn what you think I think, and yet another intermediate will be added to the chain. And in time' - his voice rose - 'there will come a generation that has got beyond facts, beyond impressions, a generation absolutely colourless, a generation

seraphically free
From taint of personality,

which will see the French Revolution not as it happened, nor as they would like it to have happened, but as it would have happened, had it taken place in the days of the Machine.'

Tremendous applause greeted this lecture, which did but voice a feeling already latent in the minds of men - a feeling that terrestrial facts must be ignored, and that the abolition of respirators was a positive gain. It was even suggested that airships should be abolished too. This was not done, because airships had somehow worked themselves into the machine's system. But year by year they were used less, and mentioned less by thoughtful men.

The second great development was the re-establishment of religion.

This, too, had been voiced in the celebrated lecture. No one could mistake the reverent tone in which the peroration had concluded, and it awakened a responsive echo in the heart of each. Those who had long worshipped silently, now began to talk. They described the strange feeling of peace that came over them when they handled the Book of the Machine, the pleasure that it was to repeat certain numerals out of it, however little meaning those numerals conveyed to the outward ear, the ecstasy of touching a button, however unimportant, or of ringing an electric bell, however superfluously.

'The Machine,' they exclaimed, 'feeds us and clothes us and houses us; through it we speak to one another, through it we see one another, in it we have our being. The Machine is the friend of ideas and the enemy of superstition: the Machine is omnipotent, eternal; blessed is the Machine.' And before long this allocution was printed on the first page of the Book, and in subsequent editions the ritual swelled into a complicated system of praise and prayer. The word 'religion' was sedulously avoided, and in theory the Machine was still the creation and the implement of man. But in practice all, save a few retrogrades, worshipped it as divine. Nor was it worshipped in unity. One believer would be chiefly impressed by the blue optic plates, through which he saw other believers; another by the mending apparatus, which sinful Kuno had compared to worms; another by the lifts, another by the Book. And each would pray to this or to that, and ask it to intercede for him with the Machine as a whole. Persecution - that also was present. It did not break out, for reasons that will be set forward shortly. But it was latent, and all who did not accept the minimum known as 'undenominational Mechanism' lived in danger of Homelessness, which means death, as we know.

To attribute these two great developments to the Central Committee, is to take a very narrow view of civilization. The Central Committee announced the developments, it is true, but they were no more the cause of them than were the kings of the imperialistic period the cause of war. Rather did they yield to some invincible pressure, which came no one knew whither, and which, when gratified, was succeeded by some new pressure equally invincible. To such a state of affairs it is convenient to give the name of progress. No one confessed the Machine was out of hand. Year by year it was served with increased efficiency and decreased intelligence. The better a man knew his own duties upon it, the less he understood the duties of his neighbour, and in all the world there was not one who understood the monster as a whole. Those master brains had perished. They had left full directions, it is true, and their successors had each of them mastered a portion of those directions. But Humanity, in its desire for comfort, had over-reached itself. It had exploited the riches of nature too far. Quietly and complacently, it was sinking into decadence, and progress had come to mean the progress of the Machine.

As for Vashti, her life went peacefully forward until the final disaster. She made her room dark and slept; she awoke and made the room light. She lectured and attended lectures. She exchanged ideas with her innumerable friends and believed she was growing more spiritual. At times a friend was granted Euthanasia, and left his or her room for the homelessness that is beyond all human conception. Vashti did not much mind. After an unsuccessful lecture, she would sometimes ask for Euthanasia herself. But the death-rate was not permitted to exceed the birth-rate, and the Machine had hitherto refused it to her.

The troubles began quietly, long before she was conscious of them.

One day she was astonished at receiving a message from her son. They never communicated, having nothing in common, and she had only heard indirectly that he was still alive, and had been transferred from the northern hemisphere, where he had behaved so mischievously, to the southern - indeed, to a room not far from her own.

'Does he want me to visit him?' she thought. 'Never again, never. And I have not the time.'

No, it was madness of another kind.

He refused to visualize his face upon the blue plate, and speaking out of the darkness with solemnity said:

'The Machine stops.'

'What do you say?'

'The Machine is stopping, I know it, I know the signs.'

She burst into a peal of laughter. He heard her and was angry, and they spoke no more.

'Can you imagine anything more absurd?' she cried to a friend. 'A man who was my son believes that the Machine is stopping. It would be impious if it was not mad.'

'The Machine is stopping?' her friend replied. 'What does that mean? The phrase conveys nothing to me.'

'Nor to me.'

'He does not refer, I suppose, to the trouble there has been lately with the music?'

'Oh no, of course not. Let us talk about music.'

'Have you complained to the authorities?'

'Yes, and they say it wants mending, and referred me to the Committee of the Mending Apparatus. I complained of those curious gasping sighs that disfigure the symphonies of the Brisbane school. They sound like some one in pain. The Committee of the Mending Apparatus say that it shall be remedied shortly.'

Obscurely worried, she resumed her life. For one thing, the defect in the music irritated her. For another thing, she could not forget Kuno's speech. If he had known that the music was out of repair -he could not know it, for he detested music - if he had known that it was wrong, 'the Machine stops' was exactly the venomous sort of remark he would have made. Of course he had made it at a venture, but the coincidence annoyed her, and she spoke with some petulance to the Committee of the Mending Apparatus.

They replied, as before, that the defect would be set right shortly.

'Shortly! At once!' she retorted. 'Why should I be worried by imperfect music? Things are always put right at once. If you do not mend it at once, I shall complain to the Central Committee.'

'No personal complaints are received by the Central Committee,' the Committee of the Mending Apparatus replied.

'Through whom am I to make my complaint, then?'

'Through us.'

'I complain then.'

'Your complaint shall be forwarded in its turn.'

'Have others complained?'

This question was unmechanical, and the Committee of the Mending Apparatus refused to answer it.

'It is too bad!' she exclaimed to another of her friends. 'There never was such an unfortunate woman as myself. I can never be sure of my music now. It gets worse and worse each time I summon it.'

'I too have my troubles,' the friend replied. 'Sometimes my ideas are interrupted by a slight jarring noise.'

'What. is it?'

'I do not know whether it is inside my head, or inside the wall.'

'Complain, in either case.'

'I have complained, and my complaint will be forwarded in its turn to the Central Committee.'

Time passed, and they resented the defects no longer. The defects had not been remedied, but the human tissues in that latter day had become so subservient, that they readily adapted themselves to every caprice of the Machine. The sigh at the crisis of the Brisbane symphony no longer irritated Vashti; she accepted it as part of the melody. The jarring noise, whether in the head or in the wall, was no longer resented by her friend. And so with the mouldy artificial fruit, so with the bath water that began to stink, so with the defective rhymes that the poetry machine had taken to emitting. All were bitterly complained of at first, and then acquiesced in and forgotten. Things went from bad to worse unchallenged.

It was otherwise with the failure of the sleeping apparatus. That was a more serious stoppage. There came a day when over the whole world - in Sumatra, in Wessex, in the innumerable cities of Courland and Brazil - the beds, when summoned by their tired owners, failed to appear. It may seem a ludicrous matter, but from it we may date the collapse of humanity. The Committee responsible for the failure was assailed by complainants, whom it referred, as usual, to the Committee of the Mending Apparatus, who in its turn assured them that their complaints would be forwarded to the Central Committee. But the discontent grew, for mankind was not yet sufficiently adaptable to do without sleeping.

'Some one is meddling with the Machine –' they began.

'Some one is trying to make himself king, to reintroduce the personal element.'

'Punish that man with Homelessness.'

'To the rescue! Avenge the Machine! Avenge the Machine!'

'War! Kill the man!'

But the Committee of the Mending Apparatus now came forward, and allayed the panic with well-chosen words. It confessed that the Mending Apparatus was itself in need of repair.

The effect of this frank confession was admirable.

'Of course,' said a famous lecturer - he of the French Revolution, who gilded each new decay with splendour - 'of course we shall not press our complaints now. The Mending Apparatus has treated us so well in the past that we all sympathize with it, and will wait patiently for its recovery. In its own good time it will resume its duties. Meanwhile let us do without our beds, our tabloids, our other little wants. Such, I feel sure, would be the wish of the Machine.'

Thousands of miles away his audience applauded. The Machine still linked them. Under the seas, beneath the roots of the mountains, ran the wires through which they saw and heard, the enormous eyes and ears that were their heritage, and the hum of many workings clothed their thoughts in one garment of subserviency. Only the old and the sick remained ungrateful, for it was rumoured that Euthanasia, too, was out of order, and that pain had reappeared among men.

It became difficult to read. A blight entered the atmosphere and dulled its luminosity. At times Vashti could scarcely see across her room. The air, too, was foul. Loud were the complaints, impotent the remedies, heroic the tone of the lecturer as he cried: 'Courage! courage! What matter so long as the Machine goes on? To it the darkness and the light are one.' And though things improved again after a time, the old brilliancy was never recaptured, and humanity never recovered from its entrance into twilight. There was an hysterical talk of 'measures,' of 'provisional dictatorship,' and the inhabitants of Sumatra were asked to familiarize themselves with the workings of the central power station, the said power station being situated in France. But for the most part panic reigned, and men spent their strength praying to their Books, tangible proofs of the Machine's omnipotence. There were gradations of terror - at times came rumours of hope - the Mending Apparatus was almost mended - the enemies of the Machine had been got under - new 'nerve-centres' were evolving which would do the work even more magnifi-cently than before. But there came a day when, without the slightest warning, without any previous hint of feebleness, the entire communication-system broke down, all over the world, and the world, as they understood it, ended.

Vashti was lecturing at the time and her earlier remarks had been punctuated with applause. As she proceeded the audience became silent, and at the conclusion there was no sound. Somewhat displeased, she called to a friend who was a specialist in sympathy. No sounds doubtless the friend was sleeping. And so with the next friend whom she tried to summon, and so with the next, until she remembered Kuno's cryptic remark, 'The Machine stops.'

The phrase still conveyed nothing. If Eternity was stopping it would of course be set going shortly.

For example, there was still a little light and air - the atmosphere had improved a few hours previously. There was still the Book, and while there was the Book there was security.

Then she broke down, for with the cessation of activity came an unexpected terror - silence.

She had never known silence, and the coming of it nearly killed her - it did kill many thousands of people outright. Ever since her birth she had been surrounded by the steady hum. It was to the ear what artificial air was to the lungs, and agonizing pains shot across her head. And scarcely knowing what she did, she stumbled forward and pressed the unfamiliar button, the one that opened the door of her cell.

Now the door of the cell worked on a simple hinge of its own. It was not connected with the central power station, dying far away in France. It opened, rousing immoderate hopes in Vashti, for she thought that the Machine had been mended. It opened, and she saw the dim tunnel that curved far away towards freedom. One look, and then she shrank back. For the tunnel was full of people - she was almost the last in that city to have taken alarm.

People at any time repelled her, and these were nightmares

from her worst dreams. People were crawling about, people were screaming, whimpering, gasping for breath, touching each other, vanishing in the dark, and ever and anon being pushed off the platform on to the live rail. Some were fighting round the electric bells, trying to summon trains which could not be summoned. Others were yelling for Euthanasia or for respirators, or blaspheming the Machine. Others stood at the doors of their cells fearing, like herself, either to stop in them or to leave them. And behind all the uproar was silence - the silence which is the voice of the earth and of the generations who have gone.

No - it was worse than solitude. She closed the door again and sat down to wait for the end. The disintegration went on, accompanied by horrible cracks and rumbling. The valves that restrained the Medical Apparatus must have been weakened, for it ruptured and hung hideously from the ceiling. The floor heaved and fell and flung her from her chair. A tube oozed towards her serpent fashion. And at last the final horror approached - light began to ebb, and she knew that civilization's long day was closing.

She whirled round, praying to be saved from this, at any rate, kissing the Book, pressing button after button. The uproar outside was increasing, and even penetrated the wall. Slowly the brilliancy of her cell was dimmed, the reflections faded from her metal switches. Now she could not see the reading-stand, now not the Book, though she held it in her hand. Light followed the flight of sound, air was following light, and the original void returned to the cavern from which it had been so long excluded. Vashti continued to whirl, like the devotees of an earlier religion, screaming, praying, striking at the buttons with bleeding hands.

It was thus that she opened her prison and escaped - escaped in the spirit: at least so it seems to me, ere my meditation closes. That she escapes in the body - I cannot perceive that. She struck, by chance, the switch that released the door, and the rush of foul air on her skin, the loud throbbing whispers in her ears, told her that she was facing the tunnel again, and that tremendous platform on which she had seen men fighting. They were not fighting now. Only the whispers remained, and the little whimpering groans. They were dying by hundreds out in the dark.

She burst into tears.

Tears answered her.

They wept for humanity, those two, not for themselves. They could not bear that this should be the end. Ere silence was completed their hearts were opened, and they knew what had been important on the earth. Man, the flower of all flesh, the noblest of all creatures visible, man who had once made god in his image, and had mirrored his strength on the constellations, beautiful naked man was dying, strangled in the garments that he had woven. Century after century had he toiled, and here was his reward. Truly the garment had seemed heavenly at first, shot with the colours of culture, sewn with the threads of self-denial. And heavenly it had been so long as it was a garment and no more, so long as man could shed it at will and live by the essence that is his soul, and the essence, equally divine, that is his body. The sin against the body - it was for that they wept in chief; the centuries of wrong against the muscles and the nerves, and those five portals by which we can alone apprehend - glozing it over with talk of evolution, until the body was white pap, the home of ideas as colourless, last sloshy stirrings of a spirit that had grasped the stars.

'Where are you?' she sobbed.

His voice in the darkness said, 'Here.'

'Is there any hope, Kuno?'

'None for us.'

'Where are you?'

She crawled towards him over the bodies of the dead. His blood spurted over her hands.

'Quicker,' he gasped, 'I am dying - but we touch, we talk, not through the Machine.'

He kissed her.

'We have come back to our own. We die, but we have recaptured life, as it was in Wessex, when Ælfrid overthrew the Danes. We know what they know outside, they who dwelt in the cloud that is the colour of a pearl.'

'But, Kuno, is it true? Are there still men on the surface of the earth? Is this - this tunnel, this poisoned darkness - really not the end?'

He replied:

'I have seen them, spoken to them, loved them. They are hiding in the mist and the ferns until our civilization stops. Today they are the Homeless - tomorrow —'

'Oh, tomorrow - some fool will start the Machine again, tomorrow.'

'Never,' said Kuno, 'never. Humanity has learnt its lesson.'

As he spoke, the whole city was broken like a honeycomb. An airship had sailed in through the vomitory into a ruined wharf. It crashed downwards, exploding as it went, rending gallery after gallery with its wings of steel. For a moment they saw the nations of the dead, and, before they joined them, scraps of the untainted sky.

SUFFER THE LITTLE CHILDREN

– STEPHEN KING

KISS SIDLEY was her name, and Teaching was her game.

She was a small woman who had to reach on tiptoes to write on the highest level of the blackboard, which she was doing now. Behind her, none of the children giggled or whispered or munched on secret sweets held in cupped hands. They knew Miss Sidley too well. Miss Sidley knew instinctively who was chewing gum at the back of the room, who had a beanshooter in his pocket, who wanted to go to the bathroom to trade baseball cards rather than use the facilities. Like God, she seemed to know everything all at once.

She was greying, and the brace she wore to support her failing back was lined clearly against her print dress. Small, constantly suffering, gimlet-eyed woman. But they feared her. Her tongue was a school-yard legend. The eyes, when turned on a giggler or a whisperer, could turn the stoutest knees to water.

Now, writing the day's list of spelling words on the slate, she reflected that the success of her long teaching career could be summed and checked and proven by this one everyday action. She could turn her back on her pupils in confidence.

'Vacation,' she said, pronouncing the word as she wrote it in her firm, no-nonsense script. 'Edward, you will please use the word vacation in a sentence.'

'I went on a vacation to New York City,' Edward piped. Then, as Miss Sidley had taught, he repeated the word carefully. 'Vay-cay-shun.'

'Very good, Edward.' She began the next word. She had her little tricks, of course; success, she firmly believed, depended as much upon taking note of little things as it did upon the big ones. She applied the principle constantly in the classroom, and it never failed.

'Jane,' she said quietly.

Jane, who had been furtively perusing her Reader, looked up guiltily

'Close that book right now, please.' The book shut; lane looked pale, hating eyes at Miss Sidley's back. 'And you will stay for fifteen minutes after the final bell.'

Jane's lips trembled. 'Yes, Miss Sidley.'

One of her little tricks was the careful use of her glasses. The whole class was reflected to her in their thick lenses and she had always been thinly amused by their guilty frightened faces when she caught them at their nasty little games.

Now she saw a phantomish, distorted Robert in the first row wrinkle his nose. She did not speak. Robert would hang himself if given just a little more rope.

Tomorrow,' she pronounced clearly. 'Robert, you will please use the word tomorrow in a sentence.' Robert frowned over the problem. The classroom was hushed and sleepy in the late September sun. The electric clock over the door buzzed a rumour of three o'clock dismissal just a half-hour away and the only thing that kept young heads from drowsing over their spellers was the silent, ominous threat of Miss Sidley's back.

'I am waiting, Robert.'

'Tomorrow a bad thing will happen,' Robert said. The words were perfectly innocuous, but Miss Sidley, with the seventh sense that all strict disciplinarians have, could sense a double meaning.

Too-mor-row,' Robert finished. His hands were folded neatly on the desk, and he wrinkled his nose again. He also smiled a tiny side-of-the-mouth smile. Miss Sidley was suddenly unaccountably sure Robert knew her little trick with the glasses.

Very well.

She began to write the next word with no comment of commendation for Robert, letting her straight body speak its own message. She watched carefully with one eye. Soon Robert would stick out his tongue or make that disgusting finger gesture, just to see if she really knew what he was doing. Then he would be punished.

The reflection was small, ghostly, and distorted. And she had all but the barest corner of her eye on the word she was writing. Robert changed.

She caught just a corner of it, just a frightening glimpse of Robert's face changing into something . . . different.

She whirled around, face white, barely noticing the protesting stab of pain in her back.

Robert looked at her blandly, questioningly. His hands were neatly folded. The first signs of an afternoon cowlick showed at the back of his head. He did not look frightened.

I have imagined it, she thought. I was looking for something, and when there was nothing, I just made something up. However –

'Robert?' she asked. She had meant to be authoritative; the unspoken demand for confession. It did not come out that way.

'Yes, Miss Sidley?' His eyes were a very dark brown, like the mud at the bottom of a slow-running stream.

'Nothing.'

She turned back to the board and a little whisper ran through the class.

'Be *quiet!*' her voice snapped. She turned again and faced them. 'Another sound and we will all stay after school with Jane!' She addressed the whole class, but looked particularly at Robert. He looked back with a child-like I-didn't-do-it innocence.

She turned to the board and began to write, not looking out of the corners of her glasses. The last half-hour dragged, and it seemed that Robert gave her a strange look on the way out. A look that said, *we have a secret, don't we?*

It wouldn't get out of her mind.

It seemed to be stuck like a tiny string of roast beef between two molars, a small thing, actually, but feeling as big as a cinderblock.

She sat down to her solitary dinner at five, poached eggs on toast, still thinking about it. She knew she was getting older and accepted the knowledge calmly. She was not going to be one of those old lady schoolteachers dragged kicking and screaming from their classrooms at the age of retirement. They reminded her of gamblers emotionally unable to leave the tables while they were losing. But *she* was not losing. She had always been a winner.

She looked down at her poached egg.

Hadn't she?

She thought of the well-scrubbed faces in her third grade classroom, and found Robert's face superimposed over them. She got up and switched on a light.

Later, just before dropping off to sleep, Robert's face floated in front of her, smiling unpleasantly in the darkness behind her lids. The face began to change –

But before she saw exactly what it was changing into, she dropped off to sleep.

Miss Sidley spent an unrestful night and the next day her temper was short. She waited, almost hoped for a whisperer, a giggler, or perhaps even a note-passer. But the class was quiet - very quiet. They all stared at her unresponsively, and it seemed that she could feel the weight of their eyes on her like blind, crawling ants.

Now stop! she told herself sternly. She paused, controlling an urge to bite her lip. She was acting like a skittish girl just out of Seminary.

Again the day seemed to drag, and she believed she was more relieved than her charges when the dismissal bell rang. The children lined up in orderly rows at the door, boys and girls by height, hands dutifully linked.

'Dismissed,' she said, and listened sourly as they shrieked down the hall and into the bright sunlight.

What was it? It was bulbous. It *shimmered and it changed and it stared at me, yes, stared and grinned and it wasn't a child at all. It was old and it was evil and –*

'Miss Sidley?'

Her head jerked up; a little oh! hiccupped involuntarily from her throat.

It was Mr Hanning. He smiled apologetically. 'Didn't mean to disturb you.'

'Quite all right,' she said, more curtly than she had intended. What had she been thinking? What was wrong with her?

'Would you mind checking the paper towels in the girls' lavatory?'

'Surely.' She got up, placing her hands against the small of her back.

Mr Hanning looked at her sympathetically. Save it, she thought. The old maid is not amused. Or even interested.

She brushed by Mr Hanning and started down the hall to the girls' lavatory. A capering group of small boys, carrying scratched and pitted baseball equipment, grew silent at the sight of her and leaked out the door, where their cries began again.

Miss Sidley looked after them resentfully, reflecting that children had been different in her day. Not more polite - children have never had time for that - and not exactly more respectful of their elders; it was a kind of hypocrisy that had never been there before. A smiling quietness around adults that had never been there before A kind of quiet contempt that was upsetting and unnerving. As if they were . . .

Hiding behind masks.

She pushed the thought away and went into the lavatory.

It was a small, tiled room with frosted glass windows, shaped like an L. The toilets were ranged along one bar, the sinks along both sides of the shorter bar.

As she checked along the paper towel containers, she caught a glimpse of her face in one of the mirrors and was startled into looking at it more closely.

God.

There was a look that hadn't been there two days before, a frightened, watching look. With sudden shock she realized that the tiny, blurred reflection in her glasses coupled with Robert's pale, respectful face had gotten inside her and was festering.

The door opened and she heard two girls come in, giggling secretly about something. She was about to turn the corner and walk out past them when she heard her own name. She turned back to the washbowls and began checking the towel holders again.

'And then he –'

Soft giggles.

'She knows, but –'

More giggles, soft and sticky as melting soap.

'Miss Sidley is –'

Slop it! Stop *that noise!*

By moving slightly she could see their shadows, made fuzzy and ill-defined by the diffuse light filtering through the frosted windows, holding on to each other with girlish glee.

Another thought crawled up out of her mind.

They knew she *was there.*

Yes, they did, the little bitches. They knew.

She would shake them. Shake them until their teeth rattled and their giggles turned to wails and she would make them admit that they knew, they knew, they –

The shadows changed.

They seemed to elongate, to flow like dripping tallow, taking on strange, hunched shapes that made Miss Sidley cringe back against the porcelain washstands, her heart swelling in her chest.

But they went on giggling.

The voices changed, no longer girlish, now sexless and soulless, and quite, quite evil. A slow, turgid sound of mindless humour that flowed around the corner to her like river mud.

She stared at the hunched shadows and suddenly screamed at them. The scream went on and on, swelling in her head until it attained a pitch of lunacy. And then she fainted. The giggling, like the laughter of demons, followed her down into darkness.

She could not, of course, tell them the truth.

Miss Sidley knew this even as she opened her eyes and looked up at the anxious faces of Mr Manning and Mrs Crossen. Mrs Crossen was holding a bottle of sharp smelling stuff under her nose. Mr Manning turned around and told the two little girls who were looking curiously at Miss Sidley to go on home now, please.

They both smiled at her, slow, we-have-a-secret smiles, and went out.

Very well. She would keep their secret. For a while. She would not have people thinking her insane. She would not have them thinking that the first feelers of senility had touched her early. She would play their game. Until she could expose their nastiness and rip it out. By the roots.

'I'm afraid I slipped,' she said calmly, sitting up and ignoring the excruciating pain in her back. 'A patch of wetness.'

'This is awful,' Mr Hanning said. 'Terrible. Are you –'

'Did the fall hurt your back, Emily?' Mrs Crossen interrupted. Mr Manning looked at her gratefully.

Miss Sidley got up, her spine screaming in her body.

'No,' she said. 'In fact, something seems to have snapped back into place. It actually feels better.'

'We can send for a –' Mr Manning began.

'No physician necessary. I'll just go on home.' Miss Sidley smiled at him coolly.

'I'll get you a taxi.'

'I always take the bus,' Miss Sidley said. She walked out.

Mr Manning sighed and looked at Mrs Crossen. 'She *does* seem more like herself -'

The next day Miss Sidley kept Robert after school. Me did nothing, so she simply accused him falsely. She felt no qualms; he was a monster, not a little boy. And she would make him admit it.

Her back was in agony. She realized Robert knew; he expected that would help him. But it wouldn't. That was another of her little advantages. Her back had been a constant pain to her for the last twelve years, and there had been times when it had been this bad -well, almost as bad - as this.

She closed the door, shutting the two of them in.

For a moment she stood still, training her gaze on Robert. She waited for him to drop his eyes. He didn't. He gazed back at her, and presently a little smile began to play around the corners of his mouth.

'Why are you smiling, Robert?' she asked softly.

'I don't know.' Robert went on smiling.

'Tell me, please, Robert.'

Robert said nothing. He went on smiling.

The outside sounds of children at play were far off, distant, dreamy. Only the hypnotic buzz of the wall clock was real.

'There's quite a few of us,' Robert said suddenly, as if he were commenting on the weather.

It was Miss Sidley's turn to be silent.

'Eleven right here in this school.' Robert went on smiling his small smile.

Quite evil, she thought, amazed. Very, incredibly evil.

'Please don't lie,' she said clearly. 'Lies only make things worse.'

Robert's smile grew wider; it became vulpine. 'Do you want to see me change, Miss Sidley?' he asked. 'Would you like to see it right out?'

Miss Sidley felt a nameless chill. 'Co away,' she said curtly. 'And bring your mother and father to school with you tomorrow. We'll get this business straightened out.' There. On solid ground again. She waited for his face to crumble, waited for the tears and the pleas to relent.

Robert's smile grew wider. He showed his teeth. 'It will be just like Show and Tell, won't it, Miss Sidley? Robert - the other Robert - he liked Show and Tell. He's still hiding 'way, 'way down in my head.' The smile curled at the corners of his mouth like charring paper. 'Sometimes he runs around... it itches. He wants me to let him out.'

'Go away,' Miss Sidley said numbly. The buzzing of the clock seemed very loud.

Robert changed.

His face suddenly ran together like melting wax, the eyes flattening and spreading like knife-struck egg yolks, nose widening and yawning, mouth disappearing. The head elongated, and the hair was suddenly not hair but straggling, twitching growths.

Robert began to chuckle.

The slow, cavernous sound came from what had been his nose, but the nose was eating into the lower half of his face, nostrils meeting and merging into a central blackness like a huge, shouting mouth.

Robert got up, still chuckling, and behind it all she could see the last shattered remains of the other Robert, howling in maniac terror, screeching to be let out.

She ran.

She fled screaming down the corridor, and the few late-leaving pupils turned to look at her with large and uncomprehending eyes.

Mr Hanning jerked open his door and looked out just as Miss Sidley plunged through the wide glass front doors, a wild, waving scarecrow silhouetted against the bright September sky.

He ran after her, Adam's apple bobbing convulsively 'Miss Sidley! Miss *Sidley!*'

Robert came out of the classroom and watched curiously.

Miss Sidley neither heard nor saw. She clattered down the walk and across the sidewalk and into the streets with her screams trailing behind her like banners. There was a huge, blatting horn and then the bus was looming over her, the bus driver's face a plaster mask of fear. Air brakes whined and hissed like dragons in flight.

Miss Sidley fell, and the huge wheels shuddered to a smoking stop just eight inches from her frail, brace-armoured body. She lay shuddering in the pavement, hearing the crowd gather around her.

She turned over and the children were staring down at her. They were ringed in a tight little circle, like mourners around an open grave. And at the head of the grave was Robert, his little face sober and solemn, ready to read the death rites and shovel the first spade of dirt over her face.

From far away, the bus driver's shaken babble: '... crazy or somethin'... my God, another half a foot...'

Miss Sidley stared numbly at the children. Their shadows covered her and blocked out the sun. Their faces were impassive. Some of them were smiling little secret smiles, and Miss Sidley knew that soon she would begin to scream again.

Then Mr Hanning broke their tight noose and shooed them away.

Miss Sidley began to sob weakly.

She did not go back to her third grade for a month. She told Mr Hanning calmly that she had not been feeling herself, and Mr Hanning suggested that she go to a reputable, ah, doctor, and discuss the matter with him. Miss Sidley agreed that this was the only sensible and rational course. She also said that if the school board wished her resignation she would tender it immediately, although it would hurt her very much. Mr Hanning, looking uncomfortable, said he doubted if that would be necessary.

The upshot of the matter was that Miss Sidley went back to her class in late October, once again ready to play the game and now knowing how to play it.

For the first week she let things go on as ever. It seemed the whole class now regarded her with hostile, shielded eyes. Robert smiled distantly at her from his first-row seat, and she did not have the courage to take him to task.

Once, while on playground duty, Robert walked over to her, holding a dodgem ball, smiling. 'There's more of us now,' he said. 'Lots, lots more.' A girl on the jungle gym looked across the playground at them and smiled, as if she had heard.

Miss Sidley smiled serenely, refusing to remember the face changing, mutating: 'Why, Robert, whatever do you mean?'

But Robert only continued smiling and went back to his game. Miss Sidley knew the time had come.

She brought the gun to school in her handbag.

It had been her brother Jim's. He had taken it from a dead German shortly after the Battle of the Bulge. Jim had been gone ten years now. She had not opened the box that held the gun in more years than that, but when she did it was still there, gleaming dully. The four clips of shells were still in the box, too, and she loaded carefully the way Jim had showed her once.

She smiled pleasantly at her class; at Robert in particular. Robert smiled back and she could see the murky alienness swimming just below his skin, muddy, full of filth.

She never cared wondering just what was impersonating Robert, but she wished she knew if the real Robert was still inside. She did not wish to be a murderess. She decided that the real Robert must have died or gone insane, living inside the dirty, crawling thing that had chuckled at her in the classroom and sent her screaming into the street. So even if he was still alive, putting him out of his misery would be a mercy.

'Today we're going to have a Test,' Miss Sidley said.

The class did not groan or shift apprehensively; they merely looked at her. She could feel their eyes, like weights. Heavy, smothering. 'It's a very special Test. I will call you down to the mimeographing room one by one and give you your Test. Then you may have a candy and go home for the day. Won't that be nice?'

They smiled empty smiles and said nothing.

'Robert, will you come first?'

Robert got up, smiling his little smile. He wrinkled his nose quite openly at her. 'Yes, Miss Sidley.'

Miss Sidley took her bag and they went down the empty, echoing corridor together, past the sleepy buzz of reciting classes coming from behind closed doors.

The mimeograph room was at the far end of the hall, past the lavatories. It had been soundproofed two years ago; the big machine was very old and very noisy.

Miss Sidley closed the door behind them and locked it.

'No one can hear you,' she said calmly. She took the gun from her bag. 'You or the gun.'

Robert smiled innocently. 'There are lots of us, though. Lots more than here.' He put one small scrubbed hand on the paper-tray of the mimeograph machine. 'Would you like to see me change, Miss Sidley?'

Before she could speak, the change began. Robert's face began to melt and shimmer into the grotesqueness beneath, and Miss Sidley shot him. Once. In the head.

He fell back against the paper-lined shelves and slid down to the floor, a little dead boy with a round black hole above the right eye.

He looked very pathetic.

Miss Sidley stood over him, breathing hard. Her scrawny cheeks were livid.

The huddled figure didn't move.

It was human.

It *was Robert.*

No!

It was all in your mind, Emily. All in your mind.

No! No, no, no!

She went back up to the room and began to lead them down, one by one. She killed twelve of them and would have killed them all if Mrs Crossen hadn't come down for a package of composition paper.

Mrs Crossen's eyes got very big; one hand crept up and clutched her mouth. She began to scream and she was still screaming when Miss Sidley reached her and put a hand on her shoulder. 'It had to be done, Margaret,' she said sadly to the screaming Mrs Crossen. 'It's terrible, but it had to. They are all monsters. I found out.'

Mrs Crossen stared at the gay-clothed little bodies scattered around the mimeograph and continued to scream.

The little girl whose hand Miss Sidley was holding began to cry steadily and monotonously.

'Change,' Miss Sidley said. 'Change for Mrs Crossen. Show her it had to be done.'

The girl continued to weep uncomprehendingly.

'Damn you, *change!*' Miss Sidley screamed. 'Dirty bitch, dirty, crawling, filthy unnatural bitch! Change! Cod damn you, *change!*' She raised the gun. The little girl cringed, and then Mrs Crossen was on her like a cat, and Miss Sidley's back gave way.

No trial.

The papers screamed for a trial, bereaved parents swore hysterical oaths against Miss Sidley, and the city sat back on its haunches in numb shock –

– *Twelve children!*

The State Legislature called for more stringent teacher examination tests, Summer Street School closed for a week of mourning, and Miss Sidley went quietly to an antiseptic madhouse in the next state. She was put in deep analysis, given the most modern drugs, introduced into daily work-therapy sessions. A year later, under strictly controlled conditions, Miss Sidley was put in an experimental encounter-therapy situation.

Buddy Jenkins was his name, psychiatry was his game. He sat behind a one-way glass with a clipboard, looking into a room which had been out fitted as a nursery. On the far wall, the cow was jumping over the moon and the mouse was halfway up the clock. Miss Sidley Sat in her wheelchair with a story book, surrounded by a group of soft, trusting, totally mindless retarded children. They smiled at her and drooled and touched her with small wet fingers while attendants at the next window watched for the first sign of an aggressive move.

For a time Buddy thought she responded well. She read aloud, stroked a girl's head, picked up a small boy when he fell over a toy block. Then she seemed to see something which disturbed her; a frown creased her brow and she looked away from the children.

'Take me away, please,' Miss Sidley said, softly and tonelessly to no one in particular.

And so they took her away. Buddy lenkins watched the children watch her go, their eyes wide and empty, but somehow deep. One smiled, and another put his fingers in his mouth slyly. Two little girls clutched each other and giggled.

That night Miss Sidley cut her throat with a bit of broken mirror-glass, and Buddy Jenkins began to watch the children.

NO KADDISH FOR WEINSTEIN

– WOODY ALLEN

***

WEINSTEIN lay under the covers, staring at the ceiling in a depressed torpor. Outside, sheets of humid air rose from the pavement in stifling waves. The sound of traffic was deafening at this hour, and in addition to all this his bed was on fire. Look at me, he thought. Fifty years old. Half a century. Next year, I will be fifty-one. Then fifty-two. Using this same reasoning, he could figure out his age as much as five years in the future. So little time left, he thought, and so much to accomplish. For one thing, he wanted to learn to drive a car. Adelman, his friend who used to play dreidel with him on Rush Street, had studied driving at the Sorbonne. He could handle a car beautifully and had already driven many places by himself. Weinstein had made a few attempts to steer his father's Chevy but kept winding up on the sidewalk.

He had been a precocious child. An intellectual. At twelve, he had translated the poems of T.S. Eliot into English, after some vandals had broken into the library and translated them into French. And as if his high I.Q. did not isolate him enough, he suffered untold injustices and persecutions because of his religion, mostly from his parents. True, the old man was a member of the synagogue, and his mother, too, but they could never accept the fact that their son was Jewish. 'How did it happen?' his father asked, bewildered. My face looks Semitic, Weinstein thought every morning as he shaved. He had been mistaken several times for Robert Redford, but on each occasion it was by a blind person. Then there was Feinglass, his other boyhood friend: A Phi Beta Kappa. A labor spy, ratting on the workers. Then a convert to Marxism. A Communist agitator. Betrayed by the Party, he went to Hollywood and became the offscreen voice of a famous cartoon mouse. Ironic.

Weinstein had toyed with the Communists, too. To impress a girl at Rutgers, he had moved to Moscow and joined the Red Army. When he called her for a second date, she was pinned to someone else. Still, his rank of sergeant in the Russian infantry would hurt him later when he needed a security clearance in order to get the free appetizer with his dinner at Longchamps. Also, while at school he had organized some laboratory mice and led them in a strike over work conditions. Actually, it was not so much the politics as the poetry of Marxist theory that got him. He was positive that collectivization could work if everyone would learn the lyrics to 'Rag Mop.' 'The withering away of the state' was a phrase that had stayed with him, ever since his uncle's nose had withered away in Saks Fifth Avenue one day. What, he wondered, can be learned about the true essence of social revolution? Only that it should never be attempted after eating Mexican food.

The Depression shattered Weinstein's Uncle Meyer, who kept his fortune under the mattress. When the market crashed, the government called in all mattresses, and Meyer became a pauper overnight. All that was left for him was to jump out the window, but he lacked the nerve and sat on a window sill of the Flatiron Building from 1930 to 1937.

'These kids with their pot and their sex,' Uncle Meyer was fond of saying. 'Do they know what it is to sit on a window sill for seven years? There you see life! Of course, everybody looks like ants. But each year Tessie - may she rest in peace - made the Seder right out there on the ledge. The family gathered round for Passover. Oy, nephew! What's the world coming to when they have a bomb that can kill more people than one look at Max Rifkin's daughter?'

Weinstein's so-called friends had all knuckled under to the House Un-American Activities Committee. Blotnick was turned in by his own mother. Sharpstein was turned in by his answering service. Weinstein had been called by the committee and admitted he had given money to the Russian War Relief, and then added, 'Oh, yes, I bought Stalin a dining-room set.' He refused to name names but said if the committee insisted he would give the heights of the people he had met at meetings. In the end he panicked, and instead of taking the Fifth Amendment, took the Third, which enabled him to buy beer in Philadelphia on Sunday.

Weinstein finished shaving and got into the shower. He lathered himself, while steaming water splashed down his bulky back. He thought, Here I am at some fixed point in time and space, taking a shower. I, Isaac Weinstein. One of God's creatures. And then, stepping on the soap, he slid across the floor and rammed his head into the towel rack. It had been a bad week. The previous day, he had got a bad haircut and was still not over the anxiety it caused him. At first the barber had snipped judiciously, but soon Weinstein realized he had gone too far. 'Put some back!' he screamed unreasonably.

'I can't,' the barber said. 'It won't stick.'

'Well, then give it to me, Dominic! I want to take it with me!'

'Once it's on the floor of the shop it's mine, Mr Weinstein.'

'Like hell! I want my hair!'

He blustered and raged, and finally felt guilty and left. Goyim, he thought. One way or another, they get you.

Now he emerged from the hotel and walked up Eighth Avenue. Two men were mugging an elderly lady. My God, thought Weinstein, time was when one person could handle that job. Some city. Chaos every place. Kant was right: The mind imposes order. It also tells you how much to tip. What a wonderful thing, to be conscious! I wonder what the people in New Jersey do.

He was on his way to see Harriet about the alimony payments. He still loved Harriet, even though while they were married she had systematically attempted to commit adultery with all the *R's* in the Manhattan telephone directory. He forgave her. But he should have suspected something when his best friend and Harriet took a house in Maine together for three years, without telling him where they were. He didn't *want to* see it - that was it. His sex life with Harriet had stopped early. He slept with her once on the night they first met, once on the evening of the first moon landing, and once to test if his back was all right after a slipped disc. 'It's no damn good with you, Harriet,' he used to complain. 'You're too pure. Every time I have an urge for you I sublimate it by planting a tree in Israel. You remind me of my mother.' (Molly Weinstein, may she rest in peace, who slaved for him and made the best stuffed derma in Chicago - a secret recipe until everyone realized she was putting in hashish.)

For lovemaking, Weinstein needed someone quite opposite. Like LuAnne, who made sex an art. The only trouble was she couldn't count to twenty without taking her shoes off. He once tried giving her a book on existentialism, but she ate it. Sexually, Weinstein had always felt inadequate. For one thing, he felt short. He was five-four in his stocking feet, although in someone else's stocking feet he could be as tall as five-six. Dr Klein, his analyst, got him to see that jumping in front of a moving train was more hostile than self-destructive but in either case would ruin the crease in his pants. Klein was his third analyst. His first was a Jungian, who suggested they try a Ouija board. Before that, he attended 'group,' but when it came time for him to speak he got dizzy and could only recite the names of all the planets. His problem was women, and he knew it. He was impotent with any woman who finished college with higher than a B-minus average. He felt most at home with graduates of typing school, although if the woman did over sixty words a minute he panicked and could not perform.

Weinstein rang the bell to Harriet's apartment, and suddenly she was standing before him. Swelling to maculate giraffe, as usual, thought Weinstein. It was a private joke that neither of them understood.

'Hello, Harriet,' he said.

'Oh, Ike,' she said. 'You needn't be so damn self-righteous.'

She was right. What a tactless thing to have said. He hated himself for it.

'How are the kids, Harriet?'

'We never had any kids, Ike.'

'That's why I thought four hundred dollars a week was a lot for child support.'

She bit her lip, Weinstein bit his lip. Then he bit her lip. 'Harriet,' he said, 'I... I'm broke. Egg futures are down.'

'I see. And can't you get help from your shiksa?'

"To you, any girl who's not Jewish is a shiksa.'

'Can we forget it?' Her voice was choked with recrimination. Weinstein had a sudden urge. to kiss her, or if not her, somebody.

'Harriet, where did we go wrong?'

'We never faced reality.'

'It wasn't my fault. You said it was north.'

'Reality is north, Ike.'

'No, Harriet. Empty dreams are north. Reality is west. False hopes are east, and I think Louisiana is south.'

She still had the power to arouse him. He reached out for her, but she moved away and his hand came to rest in some sour cream.

'Is that why you slept with your analyst?' he finally blurted out. His face was knotted with rage. He felt like fainting but couldn't remember the proper way to fall.

'That was therapy,' she said coldly. 'According to Freud, sex is the royal road to the unconscious.'

'Freud said *dreams* are the road to the unconscious.'

'Sex, dreams - you're going to nitpick?'

'Goodbye, Harriet.'

It was no use. *Rien à dire, lien à faire.* Weinstein left and walked over to Union Square. Suddenly hot tears burst forth, as if from a broken dam. Hot, salty tears pent up for ages rushed out in an unabashed wave of emotion. The problem was, they were coming out of his ears. Look at this, he thought; I can't even cry properly. He dabbed his ear with Kleenex and went home.

FEBRUARY 1999: YLLA

– RAY BRADBURY

***

THEY had a house of crystal pillars on the planet Mars by the edge of an empty sea, and every morning you could see Mrs K eating the golden fruits that grew from the crystal walls, or cleaning the house with handfuls of magnetic dust which, taking all dirt with it, blew away on the hot wind. Afternoons, when the fossil sea was warm and motionless, and the wine trees stood stiff in the yard, and the little distant Martian bone town was all enclosed, and no one drifted out their doors, you could see Mr K himself in his room, reading from a metal book with raised hieroglyphs over which he brushed his hand, as one might play a harp. And from the book, as his fingers stroked, a voice sang, a soft ancient voice, which told tales of when the sea was red steam on the shore and ancient men had carried clouds of metal insects and electric spiders into battle.

Mr and Mrs K had lived by the dead sea for twenty years, and their ancestors had lived in the same house, which turned and followed the sun, flower-like, for ten centuries.

Mr and Mrs K were not old. They had the fair, brownish skin of the true Martian, the yellow coin eyes, the soft musical voices. Once they had liked painting pictures with chemical fire, swimming in the canals in the seasons when the wine trees filled them with green liquors, and talking into the dawn together by the blue phosphorous portraits in the speaking room.

They were not happy now.

This morning Mrs K stood between the pillars, listening to the desert sands heat, melt into yellow wax, and seemingly run on the horizon.

Something was going to happen.

She waited.

She watched the blue sky of Mars as if it might at any moment grip in on itself, contract, and expel a shining miracle down upon the sand.

Nothing happened.

Tired of waiting, she walked through the misting pillars. A gentle rain sprang from the fluted pillar tops, cooling the scorched air, falling gently on her. On hot days it was like walking in a creek. The floors of the house glittered with cool streams. In the distance she heard her husband playing his book steadily, his fingers never tired of the old songs. Quietly she wished he might one day again spend as much time holding and touching her like a little harp as he did his incredible books.

But no. She shook her head, an imperceptible, forgiving shrug. Her eyelids closed softly down upon her golden eyes. Marriage made people old and familiar, while still young.

She lay back in a chair that moved to take her shape even as she moved. She closed her eyes tightly and nervously.

The dream occurred.

Her brown fingers trembled, came up, grasped at the air. A moment later she sat up, startled, gasping.

She glanced about swiftly, as if expecting someone there before her. She seemed disappointed; the space between the pillars was empty.

Her husband appeared in a triangular door. 'Did you call?' he asked irritably.

'No!' she cried.

'I thought I heard you cry out.'

'Did I? I was almost asleep and had a dream!'

'In the daytime? You don't often do that.'

She sat as if struck in the face by the dream. 'How strange, how very strange,' she murmured. 'The dream.'

'Oh?' He evidently wished to return to his book.

'I dreamed about a man.'

'A man?'

'A tall man, six feet one inch tall.'

'How absurd; a giant, a misshapen giant.'

'Somehow' - she tried the words - 'he looked all right. In spite of being tall. And he had - oh, I know you'll think it silly

- he had *blue* eyes!'

'Blue eyes! Gods!' cried Mr K. 'What'll you dream next? I suppose he had *black* hair?'

'How did you guess?' She was excited.

'I picked the most unlikely color,' he replied coldly.

'Well, black it was!' she cried. 'And he had a very white skin; oh, he was *most* unusual! He was dressed in a strange uniform and he came down out of the sky and spoke pleasantly to me.' She smiled.

'Out of the sky; what nonsense!'

'He came in a metal thing that glittered in the sun,' she remembered. She closed her eyes to shape it again. 'I dreamed there was the sky and something sparkled like a coin thrown into the air, and suddenly it grew large and fell down softly to land, a long silver craft, round and alien. And a door opened in the side of the silver object and this tall man stepped out.'

'If you worked harder you wouldn't have these silly dreams.'

'I rather enjoyed it,' she replied, lying back. 'I never suspected myself of such an imagination. Black hair, blue eyes, and white skin! What a strange man, and yet - quite handsome.'

'Wishful thinking.'

'You're unkind. I didn't think him up on purpose; he just came in my mind while I drowsed. It wasn't like a dream. It was so unexpected and different. He looked at me and he said, "I've come from the third planet in my ship. My name is Nathaniel York -"'

'A stupid name; it's no name at all,' objected the husband.

'Of course it's stupid, because it's a dream,' she explained softly. 'And he said, "This is the first trip across space. There are only two of us in our ship, myself and my friend Bert."'

'*Another* stupid name.'

'And he said, "We're from a city on *Earth;* that's the name of our planet,"' continued Mrs K. 'That's what he said. "Earth" was the name he spoke. And he used another language. Somehow I understood him. With my mind. Telepathy, I suppose.'

Mr K turned away. She stopped him with a word. 'Yll?' she called quietly. 'Do you ever wonder if - well, if there *are* people living on the third planet?'

'The third planet is incapable of supporting life,' stated the husband patiently. 'Our scientists have said there's far too much oxygen in their atmosphere.'

'But wouldn't it be fascinating if there *were* people? And they traveled through space in some sort of ship?'

'Really, Ylla, you know how I hate this emotional wailing. Let's get on with our work.' It was late in the day when she began singing the song as she moved among the whispering pillars of rain. She sang it over and over again.

'What's that song?' snapped her husband at last, walking in to sit at the fire table.

'I don't know.' She looked up, surprised at herself. She put her hand to her mouth, unbelieving. The sun was setting. The house was closing itself in, like a giant flower, with the passing of light. A wind blew among the pillars; the fire table bubbled its fierce pool of silver lava. The wind stirred her russet hair, crooning softly in her ears. She stood silently looking out into the great sallow distances of sea bottom, as if recalling something, her yellow eyes soft and moist. '"Drink to me only with thine eyes, and I will pledge with mine,"' she sang, softly, quietly, slowly. '"Or leave a kiss within the cup, and I'll not ask for wine."' She hummed now, moving her hands in the wind ever so lightly, her eyes shut. She finished the song.

It was very beautiful.

'Never heard that song before. Did you compose it?' he inquired, his eyes sharp.

'No. Yes. No, I don't know, really!' She hesitated wildly. 'I don't even know what the words are; they're another language!'

'What language?'

She dropped portions of meat numbly into the simmering lava. 'I don't know.' She drew the meat forth a moment later, cooked, served on a plate for him. 'It's just a crazy thing I made up, I guess. I don't know why.'

He said nothing. He, watched her drown meats in the hissing fire pool. The sun was gone. Slowly, slowly the night came in to fill the room, swallowing the pillars and both of them, like a dark wine poured to the ceiling. Only the silver lava's glow lit their faces.

She hummed the strange song again.

Instantly he leaped from his chair and stalked angrily from the room.

Later, in isolation, he finished supper.

When he arose he stretched, glanced at her, and suggested, yawning, 'Let's take the flame birds to town tonight to see an entertainment.'

'You don't *mean* it?' she said. 'Are you feeling well?'

'What's so strange about that?'

'But we haven't gone for an entertainment in six months!'

'I think it's a good idea.'

'Suddenly you're so solicitous,' she said.

'Don't talk that way,' he replied peevishly. 'Do you or do you not want to go?'

She looked out at the pale desert. The twin white moons were rising. Cool water ran softly about her toes. She began to tremble just the least bit. She wanted very much to sit quietly here, soundless, not moving, until this thing occurred, this thing expected all day, this thing that could not occur but might. A drift of song brushed through her mind.

'I –'

'Do you good,' he urged. 'Come along now.'

'I'm tired,' she said. 'Some other night.'

'Here's your scarf.' He handed her a phial. 'We haven't gone anywhere in months.'

'Except you, twice a week to Xi City.' She wouldn't look at him.

'Business,' he said.

'Oh?' She whispered to herself.

From the phial a liquid poured, turned to blue mist, settled about her neck, quivering.

The flame birds waited, like a bed of coals, glowing on the cool smooth sands. The white canopy ballooned on the night wind, flapping softly, tied by a thousand green ribbons to the birds.

Ylla laid herself back in the canopy and, at a word from her husband, the birds leaped, burning, toward the dark sky. The ribbons tautened, the canopy lifted. The sand slid whining under; the blue hills drifted by, drifted by, leaving their home behind, the raining pillars, the caged flowers, the singing books, the whispering floor creeks. She did not look at her husband. She heard him crying out to the birds as they rose higher, like ten thousand hot sparkles, so many red-yellow fireworks in the heavens, tugging the canopy like a flower petal, burning through the wind.

She didn't watch the dead, ancient bone-chess cities slide under, or the old canals filled with emptiness and dreams. Past dry rivers and dry lakes they flew, like a shadow of the moon, like a torch burning.

She watched only the sky.

The husband spoke.

She watched the sky.

'Did you hear what I said?'

'What?'

He exhaled. 'You might pay attention.'

'I was thinking.'

'I never thought you were a nature lover, but you're certainly interested in the sky tonight,' he said.

'It's very beautiful.'

'I was figuring,' said the husband slowly. 'I thought I'd call Hulle tonight. I'd like to talk to him about us spending some time, oh, only a week or so, in the Blue Mountains. It's just an idea – '

'The Blue Mountains!' She held to the canopy rim with one hand, turning swiftly toward him.

'Oh, it's just a suggestion.'

'When do you want to go?' she asked, trembling.

'I thought we might leave tomorrow morning. You know, an early start and all that,' he said very casually.

'But we *never* go this early in the year!'

'Just this once, I thought – ' He smiled. 'Do us good to get away. Some peace and quiet. You know. You haven't anything *else* planned? We'll go, won't we?'

She took a breath, waited, and then replied, 'No.'

'What?' His cry startled the birds. The canopy jerked.

'No,' she said firmly. 'It's settled. I won't go.'

He looked at her. They did not speak after that. She turned away.

The birds flew on, ten thousand firebrands down the wind.

In the dawn the sun, through the crystal pillars, melted the fog that supported Ylla as she slept. All night she had hung above the floor, buoyed by the soft carpeting of mist that poured from the walls when she lay down to rest. All night she had slept on this silent river, like a boat upon a soundless tide. Now the fog burned away, the mist level lowered until she was deposited upon the shore of wakening.

She opened her eyes.

Her husband stood over her. He looked as if he had stood there for hours, watching. She did not know why, but she could not look him in the face.

'You've been dreaming again!' he said. 'You spoke out and kept me awake. I *really* think you should see a doctor.'

'I'll be all right.'

'You talked a lot in your sleep!'

'Did I?' She started up.

Dawn was cold in the room. A gray light filled her as she lay there.

'What was your dream?'

She had to think a moment to remember. 'The ship. It came from the sky again, landed, and the tall man stepped out and talked with me, telling me little jokes, laughing, and it was pleasant.'

Mr K touched a pillar. Founts of warm water leaped up, steaming; the chill vanished from the room. Mr K's face was impassive.

'And then,' she said, 'this man, who said his strange name was Nathaniel York, told me I was beautiful and - and kissed me.'

'Ha!' cried the husband, turning violently away, his jaw working.

'It's only a dream.' She was amused.

'Keep your silly, feminine dreams to yourself!'

'You're acting like a child.' She lapsed back upon the few remaining remnants of chemical mist. After a moment she laughed softly. 'I thought of some more of the dream,' she confessed.

'Well, what is it, what *is* it?' he shouted.

'Yll, you're so bad-tempered.'

'Tell me!' he demanded. 'You can't keep secrets from me!' His face was dark and rigid as he stood over her.

'I've never seen you this way,' she replied, half shocked, half entertained. 'All that happened was this Nathaniel York person told me - well, he told me that he'd take me away into his ship, into the sky with him, and take me back to his planet with him. It's really quite ridiculous.'

'Ridiculous, is it!' he almost screamed. 'You should have heard yourself, fawning on him, talking to him, singing with him, oh gods, all night; you should have *heard* yourself!'

'Yll!'

'When's he landing? Where's he coming down with his damned ship?'

'Yll, lower your voice.'

'Voice be damned!' He bent stiffly over her. 'And in this dream' -he seized her wrist - 'didn't the ship land over in Green Valley, *didn't* it? Answer me!'

'Why, yes –'

'And it landed this afternoon, didn't it?' he kept at her.

'Yes, yes, I think so, yes, but only in a dream!'

'Well' – he flung her hand away stiffly - 'it's good you're truthful! I heard every word you said in your sleep. You mentioned the valley and the time.' Breathing hard, he walked between the pillars like a man blinded by a lightning bolt. Slowly his breath returned. She watched him as if he were quite insane. She arose finally and went to him. 'Yll,' she whispered.

'I'm all right.'

'You're sick.'

'No.' He forced a tired smile. 'Just childish. Forgive me, darling.' He gave her a rough pat. 'Too much work lately. I'm sorry, I think I'll lie down awhile - '

'You were so excited.'

'I'm all right now. Fine.' He exhaled. 'Let's forget it. Say, I heard a joke about Uel yesterday, I meant to tell you. What do you say you fix breakfast, I'll tell the joke, and let's not talk about all this.'

'It was only a dream.'

'Of course.' He kissed her cheek mechanically. 'Only a dream.'

At noon the sun was high and hot and the hills shimmered in the light.

'Aren't you going to town?' asked Ylla.

'Town?' He raised his brows faintly.

'This is the day you always go.' She adjusted a flower cage on its pedestal. The flowers stirred, opening their hungry yellow mouths.

He closed his book. 'No. It's too hot, and it's late.'

'Oh.' She finished her task and moved toward the door. 'Well, I'll be back soon.'

'Wait a minute! Where are you going?'

She was in the door swiftly. 'Over to Pao's. She invited me!'

'today?'

'I haven't seen her in a long time. It's only a little way.'

'Over in Green Valley, isn't it?'

'Yes, just a walk, not far, I thought I'd –' She hurried.

'I'm sorry, really sorry,' he said, running to fetch her back, looking very concerned about his forgetfulness. 'It slipped my mind. I invited Dr Nlle out this afternoon.'

'Dr Nlle!' She edged toward the door.

He caught her elbow and drew her steadily in. 'Yes.'

'But Pao -'

'Pao can wait, Ylla. We must entertain Nlle.'

'Just for a few minutes –'

'No, Ylla.'

'No?'

He shook his head. 'No. Besides, it's a terribly long walk to Pao's. All the way over through Green Valley and then past the big canal and down, isn't it? And it'll be very, very hot, and Dr Nlle would be delighted to see you. Well?'

She did not answer. She wanted to break and run. She wanted to cry out. But she only sat in the chair, turning her fingers over slowly, staring at them expressionlessly, trapped.

'Ylla?' he murmured. 'You *will* be here, won't you?'

'Yes,' she said after a long time. 'I'll be here.'

'All afternoon?'

Her voice was dull. 'All afternoon.'

Late in the day Dr Nlle had not put in an appearance. Ylla's husband did not seem overly surprised. When it was quite late he murmured something, went to a closet, and drew forth an evil weapon, a long yellowish tube ending in a bellows and a trigger. He turned, and upon his face was a mask, hammered from silver metal, expressionless, the mask that he always wore when he wished to hide his feelings, the mask which curved and hollowed so exquisitely to his thin cheeks and chin and brow. The mask glinted, and he held the evil weapon in his hands, considering it. It hummed constantly, an insect hum. From it hordes of golden bees could be flung out with a high shriek. Golden, horrid bees that stung, poisoned, and fell lifeless, like seeds on the sand.

'Where are you going?' she asked.

'What?' He listened to the bellows, to the evil hum. 'If Dr Nlle is late, I'll be damned if I'll wait. I'm going out to hunt a bit. I'll be back. You be sure to stay right here now, won't you?' The silver mask glimmered.

'Yes.'

'And tell Dr Nlle I'll return. Just hunting.'

The triangular door closed. His footsteps faded down the hill.

She watched him walking through the sunlight until he was gone. Then she resumed her tasks with the magnetic dusts and the new fruits to be plucked from the crystal walls. She worked with energy and dispatch, but on occasion a numbness took hold of her and she caught herself singing that odd and memorable song and looking out beyond the crystal pillars at the sky.

She held her breath and stood very still, waiting.

It was coming nearer.

At any moment it might happen.

It was like those days when you heard a thunderstorm coming and there was the waiting silence and then the faintest pressure of the atmosphere as the climate blew over the land in shifts and shadows and vapors. And the change pressed at your ears and you were suspended in the waiting time of the coming storm. You began to tremble. The sky was stained and coloured; the clouds were thickened; the mountains took on an iron taint. The caged flowers blew with faint sighs of warning. You felt your hair stir softly. Somewhere in the house the voice-clock sang. 'Time, time, time, time ...' ever so gently, no more than water tapping on velvet.

And then the storm. The electric illumination, the engulfments of dark wash and sounding black fell down, shutting in, forever.

That's how it was now. A storm gathered, yet the sky was clear. Lightning was expected, yet there was no cloud.

Ylla moved through the breathless summer house. Lightning would strike from the sky any instant; there would be a thunderclap, a boll of smoke, a silence, footsteps on the path, a rap on the crystalline door, and her running to answer . . .

Crazy Ylla! she scoffed. Why think these wild things with your idle mind?

And then it happened.

There was a warmth as of a great fire passing in the air. A whirling, rushing sound. A gleam in the sky, of metal.

Ylla cried out.

Running through the pillars, she flung wide a door. She faced the hills. But by this time there was nothing.

She was about to race down the hill when she stopped herself. She was supposed to stay here, go nowhere. The doctor was coming to visit, and her husband would be angry if she ran off.

She waited in the door, breathing rapidly, her hand out.

She strained to see over toward Green Valley, but saw nothing.

Silly woman. She went inside. You and your imagination, she thought. That was nothing but a bird, a leaf, the wind, or a fish in the canal. Sit down. Rest.

She sat down.

A shot sounded.

Very clearly, sharply, the sound of the evil insect weapon.

Her body jerked with it.

It came from a long way off. One shot. The swift humming distant bees. One shot. And then a second shot, precise and cold, and far away.

Her body winced again and for some reason she started up, screaming, and screaming and never wanting to stop screaming. She ran violently through the house and once more threw wide the door.

The echoes were dying away, away.

Gone.

She waited in the yard, her face pale, for five minutes.

Finally, with slow steps, her head down, she wandered about the pillared rooms, laying her hand to things, her lips quivering, until finally she sat alone in the darkening wine room, waiting. She began to wipe an amber glass with the hem of her scarf.

And then, from far off, the sound of footsteps crunching on the thin, small rocks.

She rose up to stand in the center of the quiet room. The glass fell from her fingers, smashing to bits.

The footsteps hesitated outside the door.

Should she speak? Should she cry out, 'Come in, oh, come in'?

She went forward a few paces.

The footsteps walked up the ramp. A hand twisted the door latch.

She smiled at the door.

The door opened. She stopped smiling.

It was her husband. His silver mask glowed dully.

He entered the room and looked at her for only a moment. Then he snapped the weapon bellows open, cracked out two dead bees, heard them spat on the floor as they fell, stepped on them, and placed the empty bellows gun in the corner of the room as Ylla bent down and tried, over and over, with no success, to pick up the pieces of the shattered glass. 'What were you doing?' she asked.

'Nothing,' he said with his back turned. He removed the mask.

'But the gun - I heard you fire it. Twice.'

'Just hunting. Once in a while you like to hunt. Did Dr Nlle arrive?'

'No.'

'Wait a minute.' He snapped his fingers disgustedly. 'Why, I remember now. He was supposed to visit us tomorrow afternoon. How stupid of me.'

They sat down to eat. She looked at her food and did not move her hands. 'What's wrong?' he asked, not looking up from dipping his meat in the bubbling lava.

'I don't know. I'm not hungry,' she said.

'Why not?'

'I don't know. I'm just not.'

The wind was rising across the sky; the sun was going down. The room was small and suddenly cold.

'I've been trying to remember,' she said in the silent room, across from her cold, erect, golden-eyed husband.

'Remember what?' He sipped his wine.

'That song. That fine and beautiful song.' She closed her eyes and hummed, but it was not the song. 'I've forgotten it. And, somehow, I don't want to forget it. It's something I want always to remember.' She moved her hands as if the rhythm might help her to remember all of it. Then she lay back in her chair. 'I can't remember.' She began to cry.

'Why are you crying?' he asked.

'I don't know, I don't know, but I can't help it. I'm sad and I don't know why, I cry and I don't why, but I'm crying.'

Her head was in her hands; her shoulders moved again and again.

'You'll be all right tomorrow,' he said.

She did not look up at him; she looked only at the empty desert and the very bright stars coming out now on the black sky, and far away there was a sound of wind rising and canal waters stirring cold in the long canals. She shut her eyes, trembling.

'Yes,' she said. 'I'll be all right tomorrow.'

MURDER. 1986

– P. D. JAMES

THE girl lay naked on the bed WITH a knife through her heart. That was the one simple and inescapable fact. No, not simple. It was a fact horrible in its complications. Sergeant Dolby, fighting nausea, steadied his shaking thighs against the foot of the bed and forced his mind into coherence - arranging his thoughts in order, like a child piling brick on colored brick and holding its breath against the inevitable tumble into chaos. He mustn't panic. He must take things slowly. There was a proper procedure laid down for this kind of crisis. There was a procedure laid down for everything.

Dead. That, at least, was certain. Despite the heat of the June morning the slim, girlish body was quite cold, the rigor mortis already well advanced in face and arms. What had they taught him in Detective School about the onset of rigor mortis, that inexorable if erratic stiffening of the muscles, the body's last protest against disintegration and decay? He couldn't remember. He had never been any good at the more academic studies. He had been lucky to be accepted for the Criminal Investigation Department; they had made that clear enough to him at the time. They had never ceased to make it clear. A lost car; a small breaking and entering; a purse snatch. Send Dolby. He had never rated anything more interesting or important than the petty crimes of inadequate men. If it was something no one else wanted to be bothered with, send Dolby. If it was something the C.I.D. would rather not be told about, send Dolby.

And that was exactly how this death would rate. He would have to report it, of course. But it wouldn't be popular news at Headquarters. They were overworked already, depleted in strength, inadequately equipped, forced even to employ him six years after his normal retirement age. No, they wouldn't exactly welcome this spot of trouble. And the reason, as if he didn't know it, was fixed there on the wall for him to read. The statutory notice was pasted precisely over the head of her bed.

He wondered why she had chosen that spot. There was no rule about where it had to be displayed. Why, he wondered, had she chosen to sleep under it as people once slept under a Crucifix. An affirmation? But the wording was the same as he would find on the notice in the downstairs hall, in the elevator, on every corridor wall, in every room in the Colony. The Act to which it referred was already two years old.

PRESERVATION *OF THE RACE ACT* - 1984
Control *of Interplanetary Disease*
Infection Carriers

All registered carriers of the Disease, whether or not they are yet manifesting symptoms, are required under Section 2 of the above Act to conform to the following regulations. . . .

He didn't need to read further. He knew the regulations by heart -the rules by which the Ipdics lived, if you could call it living. The desperate defense of the few healthy against the menace of the many condemned. The small injustices which might prevent the greatest injustice of all, the extinction of man. The stigmata of the Diseased: the registered number tattooed on the left forearm; the regulation Ipdic suit of yellow cotton in summer, blue serge in winter; the compulsory sterilization, since an Ipdic bred only monsters; the rule prohibiting marriage or any close contact with a Normal; the few manual jobs they were permitted to do; the registered Colonies where they were allowed to live.

He knew what they would say at Headquarters. If Dolby had to discover a murder, it would have to be of an Ipdic. And trust him to be fool enough to report it.

But there was no hurry. He could wait until he was calmer, until he could face with confidence whomever they chose to send. And there were things they would expect him to have noticed. He had better make an examination of the scene before he reported. Then, even if they came at once, he would have something sensible to say.

He forced himself to look again at the body. She was lying on her back, eyes closed as if asleep, light brown hair streaming over the pillow. Her arms were crossed over her chest as if in a last innocent gesture of modesty. Below the left breast the handle of a knife stuck out like an obscene horn.

He bent low to examine it. An ordinary handle, probably an ordinary knife. A short-bladed kitchen knife of the kind used to peel vegetables. Her right palm was curved around it, but not touching it, as if about to pluck it out. On her left forearm the registered Ipdic number glowed almost luminous against the delicate skin.

She was neatly covered by a single sheet pulled smooth and taut so that it looked as if the body had been ritually prepared for examination - an intensification of the horror. He did not believe that this childish hand could have driven in the blade with such precision or that, in her last spasms, she had drawn the sheet so tidily over her nakedness. The linen was only a shade whiter than her skin. There had been two months now of almost continuous sunshine. But this body had been muffled in the high-necked tunic and baggy trousers of an Ipdic suit. Only her face had been open to the sun. It was a delicate nut-brown and there was a faint spatter of freckles across the forehead.

He walked slowly around the room. It was sparsely furnished but pleasant enough. The world had no shortage of living space, even for Ipdics. They could live in comfort, even in some opulence, until the electricity, the television, the domestic computer, the micro-oven broke down. Then these things remained broken. The precious skills of electricians and engineers were not wasted on Ipdics. And it was extraordinary how quickly squalor could replace luxury.

A breakdown of electricity in a building like this could mean no hot food, no light, no heating. He had known Ipdics who had frozen or starved to death in apartments which, back in 1980, only six years ago, must have cost a fortune to rent. Somehow the will to survive died quickly in them. It was easier to wrap themselves in blankets and reach for that small white capsule so thoughtfully provided by the Government, the simple painless way out which the whole healthy community was willing for them to take.

But this girl, this female Ipdic PXN 07926431, wasn't living in squalor. The apartment was clean and almost obsessively neat. The micro-oven was out of order, but there was an old-fashioned electric cooker in the kitchen and when he turned it on the hot plate glowed red. There were even a few personal possessions - a little clutch of seashells carefully arranged on the window ledge, a Staffordshire porcelain figurine of a shepherdess, a child's tea service on a papier-mâché tray.

Her yellow Ipdic suit was neatly folded over the back of a chair. He took it up and saw that she had altered it to fit her. The darts under the breasts had been taken in, the side seams carefully shaped. The hand stitching was neat and regular, an affirmation of individuality, or self-respect. A proud girl. A girl undemoralized by hopelessness. He turned the harsh cotton over and over in his hands and felt the tears stinging the back of his eyes.

He knew that this strange and half remembered sweetness was pity. He let himself feel it, willing himself not to shrink from the pain. Just so, in his boyhood, he had tentatively placed his full weight on an injured leg after football, relishing the pain in the knowledge that he could bear it, that he was still essentially whole.

But he must waste no more time. Turning on his pocket radio he made his report.

'Sergeant Dolby here. I'm speaking from Ipdic Colony 865. Female Ipdic PXN 07926431 found dead. Room 18. Looks like murder.'

It was received as he had expected.

'Oh, Cod! Are you sure? All right. Hang around. Someone will be over.'

While he waited he gave his attention to the flowers. They had struck his senses as soon as he opened the door of the room, but the first sight of the dead girl had driven them from his mind. Now he let their gentle presence drift back into his consciousness. She had died amid such beauty.

The apartment was a bower of wild flowers, their delicate sweetness permeating the warm air so that every breath was an intimation of childhood summers, an evocation of the old innocent days. Wild flowers were his hobby. The slow brain corrected itself, patiently, mechanically: wild flowers had been his hobby. But that was before the Sickness, when the words flower and beauty seemed to have meaning. He hadn't looked at a flower with any joy since 1980.

1980. The year of the Disease. The year with the hottest summer for 21 years. That summer when the sheer weight of people had pressed against the concrete bastions of the city like an intolerable force, had thronged its burning pavements, had almost brought its transport system to a stop, had sprawled in checkered ranks across its parks until the sweet grass was pressed into pale straw.

1980. The year when there were too many people. Too many happy, busy, healthy human beings. The year when his wife had been alive; when his daughter Tessa had been alive. The year when brave men, traveling far beyond the moon, had brought back to earth the Sickness - the Sickness which had decimated mankind on every continent of the globe. The Sickness which had robbed him, Arthur Dolby, of his wife and daughter.

Tessa. She had been only 14 that spring. It was a wonderful age for a daughter, the sweetest daughter in the world. And Tessa had been intelligent as well as sweet. Both women in his life, his wife and daughter, had been cleverer than Dolby. He had known it, but it hadn't worried him or made him feel inadequate. They had loved him so unreservedly, had relied so much on his manhood, been so satisfied with what little he could provide. They had seen in him qualities he could never discern in himself, virtues which he knew he no longer possessed. His flame of life was meagre; it had needed their warm breaths to keep it burning bright. He wondered what they would think of him now. Arthur Dolby in 1986, looking once more at wild flowers.

He moved among them as if in a dream, like a man recognizing with wonder a treasure given up for lost. There had been no attempt at formal arrangement. She had obviously made use of any suitable container in the apartment and had bunched the plants together naturally and simply, each with its own kind. He could still identify them. There were brown earthenware jars of Herb Robert, the rose-pink flowers set delicately on their reddish stems. There were cracked teacups holding bunches of red clover, meadow buttercups, and long-stemmed daisies; jam jars of white campion and cuckoo flowers; egg cups of birdsfoot trefoil - 'eggs and bacon,' Tessa used to call it - and even smaller jars of rueleaved saxifrage and the soft pink spurs of haresfoot.

But, above all, there were the tall vases of cow-parsley, huge bunches of strong hollow-grooved stems supporting their umbels of white flowers, delicate as bridal lace, yet pungent and strong, shedding a white dust on the table, bed, and floor.

And then, in the last jar of all, the only one which held a posy of mixed flowers, he saw the Lady Orchid. It took his breath away. There it stood, alien and exotic, lifting its sumptuous head proudly among the common flowers of the roadside, the white clover, campion, and sweet wild roses. The Lady Orchid. Orchis *Purpurea.*

He stood very still and gazed at it. The decorative spike rose from its shining foliage, elegant and distinctive, seeming to know its rarity. The divisions of the helmet were wine-red, delicately veined and spotted with purple, their somber tint setting off the clear white beauty of the lip. The Lady Orchid. Dolby knew of only one spot, the fringe of a wood in old Kent County in the Southeast Province, where this flower grew wild. The Sickness had changed the whole of human life. But he doubted if it had changed that.

It was then that he heard the roar of the helicopter. He went to the window. The red machine, like a huge angry insect, was just bouncing down onto the roof landing pad. He watched, puzzled. Why should they send a chopper? Then he understood. The tall figure in the all-white uniform with its gleaming braid swung himself down from the cockpit and was lost to view behind the parapet of the roof. But Dolby recognized at once that helmet of black hair, the confident poise of the head. C.I. Kalvert. The Commissioner of the Home Security Force in person.

He told himself that it couldn't be true - that Kalvert wouldn't concern himself with the death of an Ipdic, that he must have some other business in the Colony. But what business? Dolby waited in fear, his hands clenched so that the nails pierced his palms, waited in an agony of hope that it might not be true. But it was true. A minute later he heard the strong footsteps advancing along the corridor. The door opened. The Commissioner had arrived.

He nodded an acknowledgement to Dolby and, without speaking, went over to the bed. For a moment he stood in silence, looking down at the girl. Then he said, 'How did you get in, Sergeant?'

The accent was on the third word.

'The door was unlocked, sir.'

'Naturally, Ipdics are forbidden to lock their doors. I was asking what you were doing here.'

'I was making a search, sir.'

That at least was true. He had been making a private search.

'And you discovered that one more female Ipdic had taken the sensible way out of her troubles. Why didn't you call the Sanitary Squad? It's unwise to leave a body longer than necessary in this weather. Haven't we all had enough of the stench of decay?'

'I think she was murdered, sir.'

'Do you indeed, Sergeant. And why?'

Dolby moistened his dry lips and made his cramped fingers relax. He mustn't let himself be intimidated, mustn't permit himself to get flustered. The important thing was to stick to the facts and present them cogently.

'It's the knife, sir. If she were going to stab herself, I think she would have fallen on the blade, letting her weight drive it in, then the body would have been found face downwards. That way, the blade would have done all the work. I don't think she would have had the strength or the skill to pierce her heart lying in that position. It looks almost surgical. It's too neat. The man who drove that knife in knew what he was doing. And then there's the sheet. She couldn't have placed it over herself so neatly.'

'A valid point, Sergeant. But the fact that someone considerately tidied her up after death doesn't necessarily mean that he killed her. Anything else?'

He was walking restlessly about the room as he talked, touching nothing, his hands clasped behind his back. Dolby wished that he would stand still. He said, 'But why use a knife at all, sir? She must have been issued her euthanasia capsule.'

'Not a very dramatic way to go, Dolby. The commonest door for an Ipdic to let life out. She may have exercised a feminine preference for a more individualistic death. Look around this room, Sergeant. Does she strike you as having been an ordinary girl?'

No, she hadn't struck Dolby as ordinary. But this was ground he dare not tread. He said doggedly, 'And why should she be naked, sir? Why take all her clothes off to kill herself?'

'Why, indeed. That shocks you, does it, Dolby? It implies an unpleasant touch of exhibitionism. It offends your modesty. But perhaps she was an exhibitionist. The flowers would suggest it. She made her room into a bower of fragrance and beauty. Then, naked, as unencumbered as the flowers, she stretched herself out like a sacrifice, and drove a knife through her heart. Can you, Sergeant, with your limited imagination, understand that a woman might wish to die like that?'

Kalvert swung round and strode over to him. The fierce black eyes burned into Dolby's. The Sergeant felt frightened, at a loss. The conversation was bizarre. He felt they were playing some private game, but that only one of them knew the rules.

What did Kalvert want of him? In a normal world, in the world before the Sickness when the old police force was at full strength, the Commissioner wouldn't even have known that Dolby existed. Yet here they both were, engaged, it seemed, in some private animus, sparring over the body of an unimportant dead Ipdic.

It was very hot in the room now and the scent of the flowers had been growing stronger. Dolby could feel the beads of sweat on his brow. Whatever happened he must hold on to the facts. He said, 'The flowers needn't be funeral flowers. Perhaps they were for a celebration.'

'That would suggest the presence of more than one person. Even Ipdics don't celebrate alone. Have you found any evidence that someone was with her when she died?'

He wanted to reply, 'Only the knife in her breast.' But he was silent. Kalvert was pacing the room again. Suddenly he stopped and glanced at his watch. Then, without speaking, he turned on the television. Dolby remembered. Of course. The Leader was due to speak after the midday news. It was already 12:32. He would be almost finished.

The screen flickered and the too familiar face appeared. The Leader looked very tired. Even the makeup artist hadn't been able to disguise the heavy shadows under the eyes or the hollows beneath the cheekbones. With that beard and the melancholy, pain-filled face, he looked like an ascetic prophet. But he always had. His face hadn't changed much since the days of his student protest. People said that, even then, he had only really been interested in personal power. Well, he was still under thirty, but he had it now. All the power he could possibly want. The speech was nearly over.

'And so we must find our own solution. We have a tradition in this country of humanity and justice. But how far can we let tradition hamper us in the great task of preserving our race? We know what is happening in other countries, the organized and ceremonial mass suicides of thousands of Ipdics at a time, the humane Disposal Squads, the compulsory matings between computer-selected Normals. Some compulsory measures against the Ipdics we must now take. As far as possible we have relied on gentle voluntary methods. But can we afford to fall behind while other less scrupulous nations are breeding faster and more selectively, disposing of their Ipdics, re-establishing their technology, looking with covetous eyes at the great denuded spaces of the world. One day they will be repopulated. It is our duty to take part in this great process. The world needs our race. The time has come for every one of us, particularly our Ipdics, to ask ourselves with every breath we draw: have I the right to be alive?'

Kalvert turned off the set.

'I think we can forego the pleasure of seeing once again Mrs Sartori nursing her fifth healthy daughter. Odd to think that the most valuable human being in the world is a healthy fecund female. But you got the message I hope, Sergeant. This Ipdic had the wisdom to take her own way out while she still had a choice. And if somebody helped her, who are we to quibble?'

'It was still murder, sir. I know that killing an Ipdic isn't a capital crime. But the Law hasn't altered yet. It's still a felony to kill any human being.'

'Ah, yes. A felony. And you, of course, are dedicated to the detection and punishment of felonies. The first duty of a policeman is to prevent crime; the second is to detect and punish the criminal. You learned all that when you were in Detective School, didn't you? Learned it all by heart. I remember reading the first report on you, Dolby. It was almost identical with the last. "Lacking in initiative. Deficient in imagination. Tends to make errors of judgment. Should make a reliable subordinate. Lacks self-confidence." But it did admit that, when you manage to get an idea into your head, it sticks there. And you have an idea in your head. Murder. And murder is a felony. Well, what do you propose to do about it?'

'In cases of murder the body is first examined by the forensic pathologist.'

'Not this body, Dolby. Do you know how many pathologists this country now has? We have other uses for them than to cut up dead Ipdics. She was a young female. She was not pregnant. She was stabbed through the heart. What more do we need to know?'

'Whether or not a man was with her before she died.'

'I think you can take it there was. Male Ipdics are not yet being sterilized. So we add another fact. She probably had a lover. What else do you want to know?'

'Whether or not there are prints on the knife, sir, and, if so, whose they are.'

Kalvert laughed aloud. 'We were short of forensic scientists before the Sickness. How many do you suppose we have now? There was another case of capital murder reported this morning. An Ipdic has killed his former wife because she obeyed the Law and kept away from him. We can't afford to lose a single healthy woman, can we, Dolby? There's the rumor of armed bands of Ipdics roaming the Southeast Province. There's the case of the atomic scientist with the back of his skull smashed in. A scientist, Dolby! Now, do you really want to bother the lab with this petty trouble?'

Dolby said obstinately, 'I know that someone was with her when she picked the flowers. That must have been yesterday - they're still fresh even in this heat, and wild flowers fade quickly. I think he probably came back here with her and was with her when she died.'

'Then find him, Sergeant, if you must. But don't ask for help I can't give.'

He walked over to the door without another glance at the room or at the dead girl, as if neither of them held any further interest for him. Then he turned: 'You aren't on the official list of men encouraged to breed daughters in the interest of the race, are you, Sergeant?'

Dolby wanted to reply that he once had a daughter. She was dead and he wanted no other.

'No, sir. They thought I was too old. And then there was the adverse psychologist's report.'

'A pity. One would have thought that the brave new world could have made room for just one or two people who were unintelligent, lacking in imagination, unambitious, inclined to errors of judgment. People will persist in going their own obstinate way. Goodbye, Dolby, Report to me personally on this case, will you? I shall be interested to hear how you progress. Who knows, you may reveal unsuspected talents.'

He was gone. Dolby waited for a minute as if to cleanse his mind of that disturbing presence. As the confident footsteps died away, even the room seemed to settle itself into peace. Then Dolby began the few tasks which still remained.

There weren't many. First, he took the dead girl's fingerprints. He worked with infinite care, murmuring to her as he gently pressed the pad against each fingertip, like a doctor reassuring a child. It would be pointless, he thought, to compare them with the prints on any of the ordinary objects in the room. That would prove nothing except that another person had been there. The only prints of importance would be those on the knife. But there were no prints on the knife - only an amorphous smudge of whorls and composites as if someone had attempted to told her hand around the shaft but had lacked the courage to press the fingers firm.

But the best clue was still there - the Lady Orchid, splendid in its purity and beauty, the flower which told him where she had spent the previous day, the flower which might lead him to the man who had been with her. And there was another clue, something he had noticed when he had first examined the body closely. He had said nothing to Kalvert. Perhaps Kalvert hadn't noticed it or hadn't recognized its significance. Perhaps he had been cleverer than Kalvert. He told himself that he wasn't really as stupid as people sometimes thought. It was just that his mind was so easily flustered into incoherence when stronger men bullied or taunted him. Only his wife and daughter had really understood that, had given him the confidence to fight it.

It was time to get started. They might deny him the services of the pathologist and the laboratory, but they still permitted him the use of his car. It would be little more than an hour's drive.

But, before leaving, he bent once more over the body. The Disposal Squad would soon be here for it. He would never see it again. So he studied the clue for the last time - the faint, almost imperceptible circle of paler skin round the third finger of her left hand. The finger that could have worn a ring through the whole of a hot summer day . . .

He drove through the wide streets and sun-filled squares, through the deserted suburbs, until the tentacles of the city fell away and he was in open country. The roads were pitted and unmended, the hedges high and unkempt, the fields a turbulent sea of vegetation threatening to engulf the unpeopled farmlands. But the sun was pleasant on his face. He could almost persuade himself that this was one of the old happy jaunts into the familiar and well-loved countryside of Old Kent.

He had crossed the boundary into the Southeast Province and was already looking for the remembered landmarks of hillside and church spire when it happened. There was an explosion, a crack like a pistol shot, and the windshield shattered in his face. He felt splinters of glass stinging his cheeks. Instinctively he guarded his face with his arms. The car swerved out of control and lurched onto the grass verge. He felt for the ignition key and turned off the engine. Then he tentatively opened his eyes. They were uninjured. And it was then he saw the Ipdics.

They came out of the opposite ditch and moved toward him, with stones still in their hands. There were half a dozen of them. One, the tallest, seemed to be their leader. The others shuffled at his heels, lumpy figures in their illfitting yellow suits, their feet brown and bare, their hair matted like animals', their greedy eyes fixed on the car. They stood still, looking at him. And then the leader drew his right hand from behind his back, and Dolby saw that it held a gun.

His heart missed a beat. So it was true! Somehow the Ipdics were getting hold of weapons. He got out of the car, trying to recall the exact instructions of such an emergency. Never show fear. Keep calm. Exert authority. Remember that they are inferior, unorganized, easily cowed. Never drop your eyes. But his voice, even to him, sounded feeble, pitched unnaturally high.

The possession of a weapon by an Ipdic is a capital crime. The punishment is death. Give me that gun.'

The voice that replied was quiet, authoritative, the kind of voice one used to call educated.

'No. First you give me the keys to the car. Then I give you something in return. A cartridge in your belly!'

His followers cackled their appreciation. It was one of the most horrible sounds in the world - the laughter of an Ipdic.

The Ipdic pointed the gun at Dolby, moving it slowly from

side to side as if selecting his precise target. He was enjoying his power, drunk with elation and triumph. But he waited a second too long. Suddenly his arm jerked upward, the gun leaped from his grasp, and he gave one high desolate scream, falling into the dust of the road. He was in the first spasm of an Ipdic fit. His body writhed and twisted, arched and contracted, until the bones could be heard snapping.

Dolby looked on impassively. There was nothing he could do. He had seen it thousands of times before. It had happened to his wife, to Tessa, to all those who had died of the disease. It happened in the end to every Ipdic. It would have happened to the girl on the bed, at peace now with a knife in her heart.

The attack would leave this Ipdic broken and exhausted. If he survived, he would be a mindless idiot, probably for months. And then the fits would come more frequently. It was this feature of the Disease which made the Ipdics so impossible to train or employ, even for the simplest of jobs.

Dolby walked up to the writhing figure and kicked away the gun, then picked it up. It was a revolver, a Smith and Wesson .38, old but in good condition. He saw that it was loaded. After a second's thought he slipped it into the pocket of his jacket.

The remaining Ipdics had disappeared, scrambling back into the hedges with cries of anguish and fear. The whole incident was over so quickly that it already seemed like a dream. Only the tortured figure in the dust and the cold metal in his pocket were witnesses to its reality. He should report it at once, of course. The suppression of armed Ipdics was the first duty of the Home Security Force.

He backed the car onto the road. Then, on an impulse, he got out again and went over to the Ipdic. He bent to drag the writhing figure off the road and into the shade of the hedge. But it was no good. Revolted, he drew back. He couldn't bear to touch him. Perhaps the Ipdic's friends would creep back later to carry him away and tend to him. Perhaps. But he, Dolby, had his own problem. He had a murder to solve.

Fifteen minutes later he drove slowly through the village. The main street was deserted but he could glimpse, through the open cottage doors, the garish yellow of an Ipdic suit moving in the dim interior and he could see other yellow-clad figures bending at work in the gardens and fields. None of them looked up as he passed. He guessed that this was one of the settlements which had grown up in the country, where groups of Ipdics attempted to support themselves and each other, growing their own food, nursing their sick, burying their dead. Since they made no demands on the Normals they were usually left in peace. But it couldn't last long. There was no real hope for them.

As more and more of them were overtaken by the last inevitable symptoms, the burden on those left grew intolerable. Soon they too would be helpless and mad. Then the Security Force, the Health Authorities, and the Sanitary Squads would move in, and another colony of the dispossessed would be cleaned up. And it was a question of cleaning up. Dolby had taken part in one such operation. He knew what the final horror would be. But now in the heat of the sun-scented afternoon, he might be driving through the village as he had known it in the days before the Sickness, prosperous, peaceful, sleepy, with the men still busy on the farms.

He left the car at the churchyard gate and slipping the strap of his murder bag over his shoulder, walked up the dappled avenue of elms to the south entrance. The heavy oak door with its carved panels, its massive hinges of hammered iron creaked open at his touch. He stepped into the cool dimness and smelled again the familiar scent of flowers, musty hymn books, and wood polish, saw once again the medieval pillars soaring high to the hammer beams of the room, and, straining his eyes through the dimness he glimpsed the carving on the rood screen and the far gleam of the sanctuary lamp.

The church was full of wild flowers. They were the same flowers as those in the dead girl's apartment but here their frail delicaçy was almost lost against the massive pillars and the richly carved oak. But the huge vases of cow-parsley set on each side of the chancel steps made a brave show, floating like twin clouds of whiteness in the dim air. It was a church decked for a bride.

He saw a female Ipdic polishing the brass lectern. He made his way up the aisle toward her and she beamed a gentle welcome as if his appearance were the most ordinary event in the world. Her baggy Ipdic suit was stained with polish and she wore a pair of old sandals, the soles peeling away from the uppers. Her graying hair was drawn back into a loose bun from which wisps of hair had escaped to frame the anxious, sun-stained face.

She reminded him of someone. He let his mind probe once again, painfully, into the past. Then he remembered. Of course. Miss Caroline Martin, his Sunday School superintendent. It wasn't she, of course. Miss Martin would have been over 70 at the time of the Sickness. No one as old as that had survived, except those few Tasmanian aborigines who so interested the scientists. Miss Martin, standing beside the old piano as her younger sister thumped out the opening hymn and beating time with her gloved hand as if hearing some private and quite different music. Afterward, the students had gone to their different classes and had sat in a circle around their teachers. Miss Martin had taught the older children, himself among them. Some of the boys had been unruly, but never Arthur Dolby. Even in those days he had been obedient, law-abiding. The good boy. Not particularly bright, but well-behaved. Good, dull, ineffectual. Teacher's pet.

And when she spoke it was with a voice like Miss Martin's.

'Can I help you? If you've come for Evensong services, I'm afraid it isn't until five-thirty today. If you're looking for Father Reeves, he's at the Rectory. But perhaps you're just a visitor. It's a lovely church, isn't it? Have you seen our 16th century reredos?'

'I hoped I would be in time for the wedding.'

She gave a little girlish cry of laughter.

'Dear me, you are late! I'm afraid that was yesterday! But I thought no one was supposed to know about it. Father Reeves said that it was to be quite secret really. But I'm afraid I was very naughty. I did so want to see the bride. After all, we haven't had a wedding here since —'

'Since the Act?'

She corrected him gently, like Miss Martin rebuking the good boy of the class.

'Since 1980. So yesterday was quite an occasion for us. And I did want to see what the bride looked like in Emma's veil.'

'In what?'

'A bride has to have a veil, you know.' She spoke with gentle reproof, taking pity on his masculine ignorance. 'Emma was my niece. I lost her and her parents in 1981. Emma was the last bride to be married here. That was on April 28, 1980. I've always kept her veil and headdress. She was such a lovely bride.'

Dolby asked with sudden harshness the irrelevant but necessary question.

'What happened to her bridegroom?'

'Oh, John was one of the lucky ones. I believe he has married again and has three daughters. Just one daughter more and they'll be allowed to have a son. We don't see him, of course. It wasn't to be expected. After all, it is the Law.'

How despicable it was, this need to be reassured that there were other traitors.

'Yes,' he said. 'It is the Law.'

She began polishing the already burnished lectern, chatting to him as she worked.

'But I've kept Emma's veil and headdress. So I thought I'd just place them on a chair beside the font so that this new bride would see them when she came into church. Just in case she wanted to borrow them, you know. And she did. I was so glad. The bridegroom placed the veil over her head and fixed the headdress for her himself, and she walked up the aisle looking so beautiful.'

'Yes,' said Dolby. 'She would have looked very beautiful.'

'I watched them from behind this pillar. Neither of them noticed me. But it was right for me to be here. There ought to be, someone in the church. It says in the prayer book, "In the sight of God and of this congregation." She had a small bouquet of wild flowers, just a simple mixed bunch but very charming. I think they must have picked it together.'

'She carried a Lady Orchid,' said Dolby. 'A Lady Orchid picked by her bridegroom and surrounded by daisies, clover, white campion, and wild roses.'

'How clever of you to guess! Are you a friend, perhaps?'

'No,' said Dolby. 'Not a friend. Can you describe the bridegroom?'

'I thought that you must know him. Very tall, very dark. He wore a plain white suit. Oh, they were such a handsome couple! I wished Father Reeves could have seen them.'

'I thought he married them.'

'So he did. But Father Reeves, poor man, is blind.'

So that was why he risked it, thought Dolby. But what a risk!

'Which prayer book did he use?'

She gazed at him, the milky eyes perplexed. 'Father Reeves?'

'No, the bridegroom. He did handle a prayer book, I suppose?'

'Oh yes. I put one out for each of them. Father Reeves asked me to get things ready. It was I who decorated the church. Poor dears, it wasn't as if they could have the usual printed service sheets. Emma's were so pretty, her initials intertwined with the bridegroom's. But yesterday they had to use ordinary prayer books. I chose them specially from the pews and put them on the two prayer stools. I found a very pretty white one for the bride and this splendid old book with the brass clasp for the bridegroom. It looked masculine, I thought.'

It lay on the book ledge of the front pew. She made a move to pick it up, but he shot out his hand. Then he dropped his handkerchief over the book and lifted it by the sharp edges of the binding. Brass and leather. Good for a print. And this man's palm would be moist, clammy, perhaps, with perspiration and fear. A hot day; an illegal ceremony; his mind on murder. To love and to cherish until death us do part. Yes, this bridegroom would have been nervous. But Dolby had one more question.

'How did they get here? Do you know?'

'They came by foot. At least, they walked up to the church together. I think they had walked quite a long way. They were quite hot and dusty when they arrived. But I know how they really came.'

She nodded her unkempt head and gave a little conspiratorial nod.

'I've got very good ears, you know. They came by helicopter. I heard it.'

A helicopter. He knew almost without thinking exactly who was permitted the use of a helicopter. Members of the Central Committee of Government; high ranking scientists and technicians; doctors; the Commissioner of the Home Security Force, and his Deputy. That was all.

He took the prayer book out into the sun and sat on one of the flat-topped gravestones. He set up the prayer book on its end, then unzipped his murder bag. His hands shook so that he could hardly manage the brush and some of the gray powder was spilt and blew away in the breeze. He willed himself to keep calm, to take his time. Carefully, like a child with a new toy, he dusted the book and clasp with powder, gently blowing off the surplus with a small rubber nozzle. It was an old procedure, first practiced when he was a young Detective Constable. But it still worked. It always would. The arches, whorls, and composites came clearly into view.

He was right. It was a beautiful print. The man had made no effort to wipe it clean. Why should he? How could he imagine that this particular book would ever be identified among the many scattered around the church? How could he suspect that he would ever be traced to this despised and unregarded place? Dolby took out his camera and photographed the print. There must be continuity of evidence. He must leave no room for doubt. Then he classified its characteristics, ready for checking.

There was a little delay at the National Identification Computer Center when he phoned, and he had to wait his turn. When it came he gave his name, rank, secret code, and the classification of the print. There was a moment's silence. Then a surprised voice asked, 'Is that you, Dolby? Will you confirm your code.'

He did so. Another silence.

'Okay. But what on earth are you up to? Are you sure of your print classification?'

'Yes. I want the identification for elimination purposes.'

'Then you can eliminate, all right. That's the Commissioner. Kalvert, C.I. Hard luck, Dolby! Better start again.'

He switched off the receiver and sat in silence. He had known it, of course. But for how long? Perhaps from the beginning. Kalvert. Kalvert, who had an excuse for visiting an Ipdic Colony. Kalvert, who had the use of a helicopter. Kalvert, who had known without asking that the television set in her room was in working order. Kalvert, who had been too sure of himself to take the most elementary precautions against discovery, because he knew that it didn't matter, because he knew no one would dare touch him. Kalvert, one of the four most powerful men in the country. And it was he, the despised Sergeant Dolby, who had solved the case.

He heard the angry purr of the approaching helicopter without surprise. He had reported the armed attack of the Ipdics. It was certain that Headquarters would have immediately summoned a Squad from the nearest station to hunt them down. But Kalvert would know about the message. He had no doubt that the Commissioner was keeping a watch on him. He would know which way Dolby was heading, would realize that he was dangerously close to the truth. The armed Squad would be here in time. But Kalvert would arrive first.

He waited for five minutes, still sitting quietly on the gravestone. The air was sweet with the smell of grasses and vibrating with the high-treble midsummer chant of blackbird and thrush. He shut his eyes for a moment, breathing in the beauty, taking courage from its peace. Then he got to his feet and stood at the head of the avenue of elms to wait for Kalvert.

The gold braid on the all-white uniform gleamed in the sun. The tall figure, arrogant with confidence and power, walked unhesitatingly toward him, unsmiling, making no sign. When they were three feet apart, Kalvert stopped. They stood confronting each other. It was Dolby who spoke first. His voice was little more than a whisper.

'You killed her.'

He could not meet Kalvert's eyes. But he heard his reply.

'Yes, 1 killed her. Shall I tell you about it, Sergeant? You seem to have shown some initiative. You deserve to know part of the truth. I was her friend. That is prohibited by Regulation. She became my mistress. That is against the Law. We decided to get married. That is a serious crime. I killed her. That, as you earlier explained, is a felony. And what are you going to do about it, Sergeant?'

Dolby couldn't speak. Suddenly he took out the revolver. It seemed ridiculous to point it at Kalvert. He wasn't even sure that he would be able to fire it. But he held it close to his side and the curved stock fitted comfortably to his palm, giving him courage. He made himself meet Kalvert's eyes, and heard the Commissioner laugh.

'To kill a Normal is also against the Law. But it's something more. Capital murder, Dolby. Is that what you have in mind?'

Dolby spoke out of cracked lips, 'But why? Why?'

'I don't have to explain to you. But I'll try. Have you the imagination to understand that we might have loved each other, that I might have married her because it seemed a small risk for me and would give her pleasure, that I might have promised to kill her when her last symptoms began? Can you, Sergeant Dolby, enter into the mind of a girl like that? She was an Ipdic. And she was more alive in her condemned cell than you have ever been in your life. Female Ipdic PXN

07926431 found dead. Looks like murder. Remember how you reported it, Dolby? A felony. Something to be investigated. Against the Law. That's all it meant to you, isn't it?'

He had taken out his own revolver now. He held it easily, like a man casually dangling a familiar toy. He stood there, magnificent in the sunshine, the breeze lifting his black hair. He said quietly, 'Do you think I'd let any Law on earth keep me from the woman I loved?'

Dolby wanted to cry out that it hadn't been like that at all. That Kalvert didn't understand. That he, Dolby, had cared about the girl. But the contempt in those cold black eyes kept him silent. There was nothing they could say to each other. Nothing. And Kalvert would kill him.

The Squad would be here soon. Kalvert couldn't let him live to tell his story. He gazed with fascinated horror at the revolver held so easily, so confidently, in the Commissioner's hand. And he tightened the grip on his own, feeling with a shaking finger for the trigger.

The armored car roared up to the churchyard gate. The Squad were here. Kalvert lifted his revolver to replace it in the holster. Dolby, misunderstanding the gesture, whipped up his own gun and, closing his eyes, fired until the last cartridge was spent. Numbed by misery and panic, he didn't hear the shots or the thud of Kalvert's fall. The first sound to pierce his consciousness was a wild screaming and beating of wings as the terrified birds flew high. Then he was aware of an unnatural silence, and of an acrid smell tainting the summer air.

His right hand ached. It felt empty, slippery with sweat. He saw that he had dropped the gun. There was a long mournful cry of distress. It came from behind him. He turned and glimpsed the yellow- clad figure of the female Ipdic, hand to her mouth, watching him from the shadow of the church. Then she faded back into the dimness.

He dropped on his knees beside Kalvert. The torn arteries were pumping their blood onto the white tunic. The crimson stain burst open like a flower. Dolby took off his jacket with shaking hands and thrust it under Kalvert's head. He wanted to say he was sorry, to cry out like a child that he hadn't really meant it, that it was all a mistake.

Kalvert looked at him. Was there really pity in those dulling eyes? He was trying to speak. 'Poor Dolby! Your final error of judgment.'

The last word was hiccupped in a gush of blood. Kalvert turned his head away from Dolby and drew up his knees as if easing himself into sleep. And Dolby knew that it was too late to explain now, that there was no one there to hear him.

He stood up. The Squad were very close now, three of them, walking abreast, guns at hip, moving inexorably forward in the pool of their own shadows. And so he waited, all fear past, with Kalvert's body at his feet. And he thought for the first time of his daughter. Tessa, whom he had allowed to hide from him because that was the Law. Tessa, whom he had deserted and betrayed. Tessa, whom he had sought at last, but had found too late. Tessa, who had led him unwittingly to her lover and murderer. Tessa who would never have picked that Lady Orchid. Hadn't he taught her when she was a child that if you picked a wild orchid it can never bloom again?

THE ADVENTURE OF THE SPECKLED BAND

– SIR ARTHUR CONAN DOYLE

IN glancing over my notes of the seventy-odd cases in which I have during the last eight years studied the methods of my friend Sherlock Holmes, I find many tragic, some comic, a large number merely strange, but none commonplace; for, working as he did rather for the love of his art than for the acquirement of wealth, he refused to associate himself with any investigation which did not tend towards the unusual, and even the fantastic. Of all these varied cases, however, I cannot recall any which presented more singular features than that which was associated with the well-known Surrey family of the Roylotts of Stoke Moran. The events in question occurred in the early days of my association with Holmes, when we were sharing rooms as bachelors, in Baker Street. It is possible that I might have placed them upon record before, but a promise of secrecy was made at the time, from which I have only been freed during the last month by the untimely death of the lady to whom the pledge was given. It is perhaps as well that the facts should now come to light, for I have reasons to know there are widespread rumours as to the death of Dr Grimesby Roylott which tend to make the matter even more terrible than the truth.

It was early in April, in the year '83, that I woke one morning to find Sherlock Holmes standing, fully dressed, by the side of my bed. He was a late riser as a rule, and, as the clock on the mantelpiece showed me that it was only a quarter past seven, I blinked up at him in some surprise, and perhaps just a little resentment, for I was myself regular in my habits.

'Very sorry to knock you up, Watson,' said he, 'but it's the common lot this morning. Mrs Hudson has been knocked up, she retorted upon me, and I on you.'

'What is it, then? A fire?'

'No, a client. It seems that a young lady has arrived in a considerable state of excitement, who insists upon seeing me. She is waiting now in the sitting-room. Now, when young ladies wander about the Metropolis at this hour of the morning, and knock sleepy people up out of their beds, I presume that it is something very pressing which they have to communicate. Should it prove to be an interesting case, you would, I am sure, wish to follow it from the outset. I thought at any rate that I should call you, and give you the chance.'

'My dear fellow, I would not miss it for anything.'

I had no keener pleasure than in following Holmes in his professional investigations, and in admiring the rapid deductions, as swift as intuitions, and yet always founded on a logical basis, with which he unravelled the problems which were submitted to him. I rapidly threw on my clothes, and was ready in a few minutes to accompany my friend down to the sitting-room. A lady dressed in black and heavily veiled, who had been sitting in the window, rose as we entered.

'Good morning, madam,' said Holmes cheerily. 'My name is Sherlock Holmes. This is my intimate friend and associate, Dr Watson, before whom you can speak as freely as before myself. Ha, I am glad to see that Mrs Hudson has had the good sense to light the fire. Pray draw up to it, and I shall order you a cup of hot coffee, for I observe that you are shivering.'

'It is not cold which makes me shiver,' said the woman in a low voice, changing her seat as requested.

'What then?'

'It is fear, Mr Holmes. It is terror,' She raised her veil as she spoke, and we could see that she was indeed in a pitiable state of agitation, her face all drawn and grey, with restless, frightened eyes, like those of some hunted animal. Her features and figure were those of a woman of thirty, but her hair was shot with premature grey, and her expression was weary and haggard. Sherlock Holmes ran her over with one of his quick, all-comprehensive glances.

'You must not fear,' said he soothingly, bending forward and patting her forearm. 'We shall soon set matters right, I have no doubt. You have come in by train this morning, I see.'

'You know me, then?'

'No, but I observe the second half of a return ticket in the palm of your left glove. You must have started early, and yet you had a good drive in a dog-cart, along heavy roads, before you reached the station.'

The lady gave a violent start, and stared in bewilderment at my companion.

There is no mystery, my dear madam,' said he, smiling. The left arm of your jacket is spattered with mud in no less than seven places. The marks are perfectly fresh. There is no vehicle save a dog-cart which throws up mud in that way, and then only when you sit on the left-hand side of the driver.'

'Whatever your reasons may be, you are perfectly correct,' said she. 'I started from home before six, reached Leatherhead at twenty past, and came in by the first train to Waterloo. Sir, I can stand this strain no longer, I shall go mad if it continues, I have no one to turn to - none, save only one, who cares for me, and he, poor fellow, can be of little aid. I have heard of you, Mr Holmes; I have heard of you from Mrs Farintosh, whom you helped in the hour of her sore need. It was from her that I had your address. Oh, sir, do you think you could help me too, and at least throw a little light through the dense darkness which surrounds me? At present it is out of my power to reward you for your services, but in a month or two I shall be married, with the control of my own income, and then at least you shall not find me ungrateful.'

Holmes turned to his desk, and unlocking it, drew out a small casebook which he consulted.

'Farintosh,' said he. 'Ah, yes, I recall the case; it was concerned with an opal tiara. I think it was before your time, Watson. I can only say, madam, that I shall be happy to devote the same care to your case as I did to that of your friend. As to reward, my profession is its reward; but you are at liberty to defray whatever expenses I may be put to, at the time which suits you best. And now I beg that you will lay before us everything that may help us in forming an opinion upon the matter.'

'Alas!' replied our visitor. The horror of my situation lies in the fact that my fears are so vague, and my suspicions depend so entirely upon small points, which might seem trivial to another, that even he to whom of all others I have a right to look for help and advice looks upon all that I tell him about it as the fancies of a nervous woman. He does not say so, but

I can read it from his soothing answers and averted eyes. But I have heard, Mr Holmes, that you can see deeply into the manifold wickedness of the human heart. You may advise me how to walk amid the dangers which encompass me.'

'I am all attention, madam.'

'My name is Helen Stoner, and I am living with my stepfather, who is the last survivor of one of the oldest Saxon families in England, the Roylotts of Stoke Moran, on the western border of Surrey.'

Holmes nodded his head. 'The name is familiar to me,' said he.

'The family was at one time among the richest in England, and the estate extended over the borders into Berkshire in the north, and Hampshire in the west. In the last century, however, four successive heirs were of a dissolute and wasteful disposition, and the family ruin was eventually completed by a gambler, in the days of the Regency. Nothing was left, save a few acres of ground and the two-hundred-year-old house, which is itself crushed under a heavy mortgage. The last squire dragged out his existence there, living the horrible life of an aristocratic pauper; but his only son, my stepfather, seeing that he must adapt himself to the new conditions, obtained an advance from a relative, which enabled him to take a medical degree, and went out to Calcutta, where, by his professional skill and his force of character, he established a large practice. In a fit of anger, however, caused by some robberies which had been perpetrated in the house, he beat his native butler to death, and narrowly escaped a capital sentence. As it was, he suffered a long term of imprisonment, and afterwards returned to England a morose and disappointed man.

'When Dr Roylott was in India he married my mother, Mrs Stoner, the young widow of Major-General Stoner, of the Bengal Artillery. My sister Julia and I were twins, and we were only two years old at the time of my mother's remarriage. She had a considerable sum of money, not less than a thousand a year, and this she bequeathed to Dr Roylott entirely whilst we resided with him, with a provision that a certain annual sum should be allowed to each of us in the event of our marriage. Shortly after our return to England my mother died - she was killed eight years ago in a railway accident near Crewe. Dr Roylott then abandoned his attempts to establish himself in practice in London, and took us to live with him in the ancestral house at Stoke Moran. The money which my mother had left was enough for all our wants, and there seemed no obstacle to our happiness.

'But a terrible change came over our stepfather about this time. Instead of making friends and exchanging visits with our neighbours, who had at first been overjoyed to see a Roylott of Stoke Moran back in the old family seat, he shut himself up in his house, and seldom came out save to indulge in ferocious quarrels with whoever might cross his path. Violence of temper approaching to mania has been hereditary in the men of the family, and in my stepfather's case it had, I believe, been intensified by his long residence in the tropics. A series of disgraceful brawls took place, two of which ended in the police-court, until at last he became the terror of the village and the folks would fly at his approach, for he is a man of immense strength, and absolutely uncontrollable in his anger.

'Last week he hurled the local backsmith over a parapet into *a* stream, and it was only by paying over all the money that I could gather together that I was able to avert another public exposure. He had no friends at all save the wandering gipsies, and he would give these vagabonds leave to encamp upon the few acres of bramble-covered land which represent the family estate, and would accept in return the hospitality of their tents, wandering away with them sometimes for weeks on end. He has a passion also for Indian animals, which are sent over to him by a correspondent, and he has at this moment a cheetah and a baboon, which wander freely over his grounds, and are feared by the villagers almost as much as their master.

'You can imagine from what I say that my poor sister Julia and I had no great pleasure in our lives. No servant would stay with us, and for a long time we did all the work of our house. She was but thirty at the time of her death, and yet her hair had already begun to whiten, even as mine has.'

'Your sister is dead, then?'

'She died just two years ago, and it is of her death that I wish to speak to you. You can understand that, living the life which I desribed, we were little likely to see anyone of our own age and position. We had, however, an aunt, my mother's maiden sister, Miss Honoria Westphail, who lives near Harrow, and we were occasionally allowed to pay short visits at this lady's house. Julia went there at Christmas two years ago, and met there a half-pay Major of Marines, to whom she became engaged. My stepfather learned of the engagement when my sister returned, and offered no objection to the marriage; but within a fortnight of the day which had been fixed for the wedding, the terrible event occurred which has deprived me of my only companion.'

Sherlock Holmes had been leaning back in his chair with his eyes closed, and his head sunk in a cushion, but he half-opened his lids now, and glanced across at his visitor.

'Pray be precise as to details,' said he.

'It is easy for me to be so, for every event of that dreadful time is seared into my memory. The manor house is, as I have already said, very old, and only one wing is now inhabited. The bedrooms in this wing are on the ground floor, the sitting-rooms being in the central block of the buildings. Of these bedrooms, the first is Dr Roylott's, the second my sister's, and the third my own. There is no communication between them, but they all open out into the same corridor. Do I make myself plain?'

'Perfectly so.'

'The windows of the three rooms open out upon the lawn. The fatal night Dr Roylott had gone to his room early, though we knew that he had not retired to rest, for my sister was troubled by the smell of the strong Indian cigars which it was his custom to smoke. She left her room, therefore, and came into mine, where she sat for some time, chatting about her approaching wedding. At eleven o'clock she rose to leave me, but she paused at the door and looked back.

'"Tell me, Helen," said she, "have you ever heard anyone whistle in the dead of the night?"

'"Never," said I.

'"I suppose that you could not possibly whistle yourself in your sleep?"

'"Certainly not. But why?"

'"Because during the last few nights I have always, about three in the morning, heard a low clear whistle. I am a light sleeper, and it has awakened me. I cannot tell where it came from - perhaps from the next room, perhaps from the lawn. I thought that I would just ask you whether you had heard it."

'"No, I have not. It must be those wretched gipsies in the plantation."

'"Very likely. And yet if it were on the lawn I wonder that you did not hear it also."

'"Ah, but I sleep more heavily than you."

'"Well, it is of no great consequence at any rate," she smiled back at me, closed my door, and a few moments later I heard her key turn in the lock.'

'Indeed,' said Holmes. 'Was it your custom always to lock yourselves in at night?'

'Always.'

'And why?'

'I think that I mentioned to you that the Doctor kept a cheetah and a baboon. We had no feeling of security unless our doors were locked.'

'Quite so. Pray proceed with your statement.'

'I could not sleep that night. A vague feeling of impending misfortune impressed me. My sister and I, you will recollect, were twins, and you know how subtle are the links which bind two souls which are so closely allied. It was a wild night. The wind was howling outside, and the rain was beating and splashing against the windows. Suddenly, amidst all the hubbub of the gale, there burst forth the wild scream of a terrified woman. I knew that it was my sister's voice. I sprang from my bed, wrapped a shawl round me, and rushed into the corridor. As I opened my door I seemed to hear a low whistle, such as my sister described, and a few moments later a clanging sound, as if a mass of metal had fallen. As I ran down the passage my sister's door was unlocked, and revolved slowly upon its hinges. I stared at it horror-stricken, not knowing what was about to issue from it. By the light of the corridor lamp I saw my sister appear at the opening, her face blanched with terror, her hands groping for help, her whole figure swaying to and fro like that of a drunkard. I ran to her and threw my arms around her, but at that moment her knees seemed to give way and she fell to the ground. She writhed as one who is in terrible pain, and her limbs were dreadfully convulsed. At first I thought that she had not recognized me, but as I bent over her she suddenly shrieked out in a voice which I shall never forget, "0, my Cod! Helen! It was the band! The speckled band!" There was something else which she would fain have said, and she stabbed with her finger into the air in the direction of the Doctor's room, but a fresh convulsion seized her and choked her words. I rushed out, calling loudly for my stepfather, and I met him hastening from his room in his dressing-gown. When he reached my sister's side she was unconscious, and though he poured brandy down her throat, and sent for medical aid from the village, all efforts were in vain, for she slowly sank and died without having recovered her consciousness. Such was the dreadful end of my beloved sister.'

'One moment,' said Holmes; 'are you sure about this whistle and metallic sound? Could you swear to it?'

'That was what the county coroner asked me at the inquiry. It is my strong impression that I heard it, and yet among the crash of the gale, and the creaking of an old house, I may possibly have been deceived.'

'Was your sister dressed?'

'No, she was in her nightdress. In her right hand was found the charred stump of a match, and in her left a match-box.'

'Showing that she had struck a light and looked about her when the alarm took place. That is important. And what conclusions did the coroner come to?'

'He investigated the case with great care, for Dr Roylott's conduct had long been notorious in the county, but he was unable to find any satisfactory cause of death. My evidence showed that the door had been fastened upon the inner side, and the windows were blocked by old fashioned shutters with broad iron bars, which were secured every night. The walls were carefully sounded, and were shown to be quite solid all round, and the flooring was also thoroughly examined, with the same result. The chimney is wide, but is barred up by four large staples. It is certain, therefore, that my sister was quite alone when she met her end. Besides, there were no marks of any violence upon her.'

'How about poison?'

'The doctors examined her for it, but without success.'

'What do you think that this unfortunate lady died of, then?'

'It is my belief that she died of pure fear and nervous shock, though what is was which frightened her I cannot imagine.'

'Were there gipsies in the plantation at the time?'

'Yes, there are nearly always some there.'

'Ah, and what did you gather from this allusion to a band - a speckled band?'

'Sometimes I have thought that it was merely the wild talk of delirium, sometimes that it may have referred to some band of people, perhaps to these very gipsies in the plantation. I do not know whether the spotted handkerchiefs which so many of them wear over their heads might have suggested the strange adjective which she used.'

Holmes shook his head like a man who is far from being satisfied.

'These are very deep waters,' said he: 'pray go on with your narrative.'

'Two years have passed since then, and my life has been until lately lonelier than ever. A month ago, however, a dear friend, whom I have known for many years, has done me the honour to ask my hand in marriage. His name is Armitage - Percy Armitage - the second son of Mr Armitage, of Crane Water, near Reading. My stepfather has offered no opposition to the match, and we are to be married in the course of the spring. Two days ago some repairs were started in the west wing of the building, and my bedroom wall has been pierced, so that I have had to move into the chamber in which my sister died, and to sleep in the very bed in which she slept. Imagine, then, my thrill of terror when last night, as I lay awake, thinking over her terrible fate, I suddenly heard in the silence of the night the low whistle which had been the herald of her own death. I sprang up and lit the lamp, but nothing was to be seen in the room. I was too shaken to go to bed again, however, so I dressed, and as soon as it was daylight I slipped down, got a dog-cart at the Crown Inn, which is opposite, and drove to Leatherhead, from whence I have come on this morning, with the one object of seeing you and asking your advice.'

'You have done wisely,' said my friend. 'But have you told me all?'

'Yes, all.'

'Miss Roylott, you have not. You are screening your stepfather.'

'Why, what do you mean?'

For answer Holmes pushed back the frill of black lace which fringed the hand that lay upon our visitor's knee. Five little livid spots, the marks of four fingers and a thumb, were printed upon the white wrist.

'You have been cruelly used,' said Holmes.

The lady coloured deeply, and covered over her injured wrist. 'He is a hard man,' she said, 'and perhaps he hardly knows his own strength.'

There was a long silence, during which Holmes leaned his chin upon his hands and stared into the crackling fire.

'This is very deep business,' he said at last. 'There are a thousand details which I should desire to know before I decide upon our course of action. Yet we have not a moment to lose. It we were to come to Stoke Moran today, would it be possible for us to see over these rooms without the knowledge of your stepfather?'

'As it happens, he spoke of coming into town today upon some important business. It is probable that he will be away all day, and that there would be nothing to disturb you. We have a housekeeper now, but she is old and foolish, and I could easily get her out of the way.'

'Excellent. You are not averse to this trip, Watson?'

'By no means.'

'Then we shall both come. What are you going to do yourself?'

'I have one or two things which I would wish to do now that I am in town. But I shall return by the twelve o'clock train, so as to be there in time for your coming.'

'And you may expect us early in the afternoon. I have myself some small business matters to attend to. Will you not wait and breakfast?'

'No, I must go. My heart is lightened already since I have confided my trouble to you. I shall look forward to seeing you again this afternoon.' She dropped her thick black veil over her face, and glided from the room.

'And what do you think of it all, Watson?' asked Sherlock Holmes, leaning back in his chair.

'It seems to me to be a most dark and sinister business.'

'Dark enough and sinister enough.'

'Yet if the lady is correct in saying that the flooring and walls are sound, and that the door, window and chimney are impassable, then her sister must have been undoubtedly alone when she met her mysterious end.'

'What becomes, then, of these nocturnal whistles, and what of the very peculiar words of the dying woman?'

'I cannot think.'

'When you combine the ideas of whistles at night, the presence of a band of gipsies who are on intimate terms with this old doctor, the fact that we have every reason to believe that the doctor has an interest in preventing his stepdaughter's marriage, the dying allusion to a band, and finally, the fact that Miss Helen Stoner heard a metallic clang, which might have been caused by one of these metal bars which secured the shutters falling back into its place, I think there is good ground to think that the mystery may be cleared along these lines.'

'But what, then, did the gipsies do?'

'I cannot imagine.'

'I see many objections to any such a theory.'

'And so do I. It is precisely for that reason that we are going to Stoke Moran this day. I want to see whether the objections are fatal, or if they may be explained away. But what, in the name of the devil!'

The ejaculation had been drawn from my companion by the fact that our door had been suddenly dashed open, and that a huge man framed himself in the aperture. His costume was a peculiar mixture of the professional and of the agricultural, having a black top hat, a long frock-coat, and a pair of high gaiters, with a hunting-crop swinging in his hand. So tall was he that his hat actually brushed the cross-bar of the doorway, and his breadth seemed to span it across from side to side. A large face, seared with a thousand wrinkles, burned yellow with the sun and marked with every evil passion, was turned from one to the other of us, while his deep-set, bile-shot eyes, and the high, thin, fleshless nose gave him somewhat the resemblance to a fierce old bird of prey.

'Which of you is Holmes?' asked this apparition.

'My name, sir, but you have the advantage of me,' said my companion quietly.

'I am Dr Grimesby Roylott, of Stoke Moran.'

'Indeed, Doctor,' said Holmes blandly. 'Pray take a seat.'

'I will do nothing of the kind. My stepdaughter has been here. I have traced her. What has she been saying to you?'

'It is a little cold for the time of the year,' said Holmes.

'What has she been saying to you?' screamed the old man furiously.

'But I have heard that the crocuses promise well,' continued my companion imperturbably.

'Ha! You put me off, do you?' said our new visitor, taking a step forward, and shaking his hunting-crop. 'I know you, you scoundrel! I have heard of you before. You are Holmes the meddler.'

My friend smiled.

'Holmes the busybody!'

His smile broadened.

'Holmes the Scotland-yard Jack-in-office.'

Holmes chuckled heartily. 'Your conversation is most entertaining,' said he. 'When you go out close the door, for there is a decided draught.'

'I will go when I have had my say. Don't you dare meddle with my affairs. I know that Miss Stoner has been here - I traced her! I am a dangerous man to fall foul of! See here.' He stepped swiftly forward, seized the poker, and bent it into a curve with his huge brown hands.

'See that you keep yourself out of my grip,' he snarled, and, hurling the twisted poker into the fireplace, he strode out of the room.

'He seems a very amiable person,' said Holmes, laughing. 'I am not quite so bulky, but if he had remained I might have shown him that my grip was not much more feeble than his own.' As he spoke he picked up the steel poker, and with a sudden effort straightened it out again.

'Fancy his having the insolence to confound me with the official detective force! This incident gives zest to our investigation, however, and I only trust that our little friend will not suffer from her imprudence in allowing this brute to trace her. And now, Watson, we shall order breakfast, and afterwards I shall walk down to Doctors' Commons, where I hope to get some data which may help us in this matter.'

It was nearly one o'clock when Sherlock Holmes returned from his excursion. He held in his hand a sheet of blue paper, scrawled over with notes and figures.

'I have seen the will of the deceased wife,' said he. 'To determine its exact meaning I have been obliged to work out the present prices of the investments with which it is concerned. The total income, which at the time of the wife's death was little short of £1,100, is now through the fall in agricultural prices not more than £750. Each daughter can claim an income of £250, in case of marriage. It is evident, therefore, that if both girls had married this beauty would have had a mere pittance, while even one of them would cripple him to a serious extent. My morning's work has not been wasted, since it has proved that he has the very strongest motives for standing in the way of anything of the sort. And now, Watson, this is too serious for dawdling, especially as the old man is aware that we are interesting ourselves in his affairs, so if you are ready we shall call a cab and drive to Waterloo. I should be very much obliged if you would slip your revolver into your pocket. An Eley's No. 2 is an excellent argument with gentlemen who can twist steel pokers into knots. That and a tooth-brush are, I think, all that we need.'

At Waterloo we were fortunate in catching a train for Leatherhead, where we hired a trap at the station inn, and drove for four or five miles through the lovely Surrey lanes. It was a perfect day, with a bright sun and a few fleecy clouds in the heavens. The trees and wayside hedges were just throwing out their first green shoots, and the air was full of the pleasant smell of the moist earth. To me at least there was a strange contrast between the sweet promise of the spring and this sinister quest upon which we were engaged. My companion sat in front of the trap, his arms folded, his hat pulled down over his eyes, and his chin sunk upon his breast, buried in the deepest thought. Suddenly, however, he started, tapped me on the shoulder, and pointed over the meadows.

'Look there!' said he.

A heavily-timbered park stretched up in a gentle slope, thickening into a grove at the highest point. From amidst the branches there jutted out the grey gables and high rooftree of a very old mansion.

'Stoke Moran?' said he.

'Yes, sir, that be the house of Dr Grimesby Roylott,' remarked the driver.

'There is some building going on there,' said Holmes; 'that is where we are going.'

'There's the village,' said the driver, pointing to a cluster of roofs some distance to the left; 'but if you want to get to the house, you'll find it shorter to go over this stile, and so by the foot-path over the fields. There it is, where the lady is walking.'

'And the lady, I fancy, is Miss Stoner,' observed Holmes, shading his eyes. 'Yes, I think we had better do as you suggest.'

We got off, paid our fare, and the trap rattled back on its way to Leatherhead.

'I thought it as well,' said Holmes, as we climbed the stile, 'that this fellow should think we had come here as architects, or on some definite business. It may stop his gossip. Good afternoon, Miss Stoner. You see that we have been as good as our word.'

Our client of the morning had hurried forward to meet us with a face which spoke her joy. 'I have been waiting so eagerly for you,' she cried, shaking hands with us warmly. 'All has turned out splendidly. Dr Roylott has gone to town, and it is unlikely that he will be back before evening.'

'We have had the pleasure of making the Doctor's acquaintance,' said Holmes, and in a few words he sketched out what had occurred. Miss Stoner turned white to the lips as she listened.

'Good heavens!' she cried, 'he has followed me, then.'

'So it appears!'

'He is so cunning that I never know when I am safe from him. What will he say when he returns?'

'He must guard himself, for he may find that there is someone more cunning than himself upon his track. You must lock yourself from him tonight. If he is violent, we shall take you away to your aunt's at Harrow. Now, we must make the best use of our time, so kindly take us at once to the rooms which we are to examine.'

The building was of grey, lichen-blotched stone, with a high central portion, and two curving wings, like the claws of a crab, thrown out on each side. In one of these wings the windows were broken, and blocked with wooden boards, while the roof was partly caved in, a picture of ruin. The central portion was in little better repair, but the right-hand block was comparatively modern, and the blinds in the windows, with the blue smoke curling up from the chimneys, showed that this was where the family resided. Some scaffolding had been erected against the end wall, and the stonework had been broken into, but there were no signs of any workmen at the moment of our visit. Holmes walked slowly up and down the ill-trimmed lawn, and examined with deep attention the outsides of the windows.

'This, I take it, belongs to the room in which you used to sleep, the centre one to your sister's, and the one next to the main building to Dr Roylott's chamber?'

'Exactly so. But I am now sleeping in the middle one.'

'Pending the alterations, as I understand. By the way, there does not seem to be any pressing need for repairs at the end wall.'

'There were none. I believe that it was an excuse to move me from my room.'

'Ah! that is suggestive. Now, on the other side of this narrow wing runs the corridor from which these three rooms open. There are windows in it, of course?'

'Yes, but very small ones. Too narrow for anyone to pass through.'

'As you both locked your doors at night, your rooms were unapproachable from that side. Now, would you have the kindness to go into your room, and to bar your shutters.'

Miss Stoner did so, and Holmes, after a careful examination through the open window, endeavoured in every way to force the shutter open, but without success. There was no slit through which a knife could be passed to raise the bar. Then with his lens he tested the hinges, but they were of solid iron, built firmly into the massive masonry. 'Hum!' said he, scratching his chin in some perplexity, 'my theory certainly presents some difficulty. No one could pass these shutters if they were bolted. Well, we shall see if the inside throws any light upon the matter.'

A small side-door led into the white-washed corridor from which the three bedrooms opened. Holmes refused to examine the third chamber, so we passed at once to the second, that in which Miss Stoner was now sleeping, and in which her sister had met her fate. It was a homely little room, with a low ceiling and a gaping fireplace, after the fashion of old country houses. A brown chest of drawers stood in one corner, a narrow white-counterpaned bed in another, and a dressing-table on the left-hand side of the window. These articles, with two small wickerwork chairs, made up all the furniture in the room, save for a square of Wilton carpet in the centre. The boards round and the panelling of the walls were brown, worm-eaten oak, so old and discoloured that it may have dated from the original building of the house. Holmes drew one of the chairs into a corner and sat silent, while his eyes travelled round and round and up and down, taking in every detail of the apartment.

'Where does that bell communicate with?' he asked at last, pointing to a thick bell-rope which hung down beside the bed, the tassel actually lying upon the pillow.

'It goes to the housekeeper's room.'

'It looks newer than the other things?'

'Yes, it was only put there a couple of years ago.'

'Your sister asked for it, I suppose?'

'No, I never heard of her using it. We used always to get what we wanted for ourselves.'

'Indeed, it seemed unnecessary to put so nice a bell-pull there. You will excuse me for a few minutes while I satisfy myself as to this floor.' He threw himself down upon his face with his lens in his hand, and crawled swiftly backwards and forwards, examining minutely the cracks between the boards. Then he did the same with the woodwork with which the chamber was panelled. Finally he walked over to the bed and spent some time in staring at it, and in running his eye up and down the wall. Finally he took the bell-rope in his hand and gave it a brisk tug.

'Why, it's a dummy,' said he.

'Won't it ring?'

'No, it is not even attached to a wire. This is very interesting. You can see now that is is fastened to a hook just above where the little opening of the ventilator is.'

'How very absurd! I never noticed that before.'

'Very strange!' muttered Holmes, pulling at the rope. 'There are one or two very singular points about this room. For example, what a fool a builder must be to open a ventilator in another room, when, with the same trouble, he might have communicated with the outside air!'

'That is also quite modern,' said the lady.

'Done about the same time as the bell-rope,' remarked Holmes'

'Yes, there were several little changes carried out about that time.'

'They seem to have been of a most interesting character - dummy bell-ropes, and ventilators which do not ventilate. With your permission, Miss Stoner, we shall now carry our researches into the inner apartment.'

Dr Grimesby Roylott's chamber was larger than that of his stepdaughter, but was as plainly furnished. A camp bed, a small wooden shelf full of books, mostly of a technical character, an arm chair beside the bed, a plain wooden chair against the wall, a round table, and a large iron safe were the principal things which met the eye. Holmes walked slowly round and examined each and all of them with the keenest interest.

'What's in here?' he asked, tapping the safe.

'My stepfather's business papers.'

'Oh! you have seen inside, then!'

'Only once, some years ago. I remember that it was full of papers.'

'There isn't a cat in it, for example?'

'No. What a strange idea!'

'Well, look at this!' He took up a small saucer of milk which stood on the top of it.

'No; we don't keep a cat. But there is a cheetah and a baboon.'

'Ah, yes, of course! Well, a cheetah is just a big cat, and

yet a saucer of milk does not go very far in satisfying its wants, I dare say. There is one point which I should wish to determine.' He squatted down in front of the wooden chair, and examined the seat of it with the greatest attention.

'Thank you. That is quite settled,' said he, rising and putting his lens in his pocket. 'Hullo! here is something interesting!'

The object which had caught his eye was a small dog lash hung on one corner of the bed. The lash, however, was curled upon itself, and tied so as to make a loop of whipcord.

'What do you make of that, Watson?'

'It's a common enough lash. But I don't know why it should be tied.'

'That is not quite so common, is it? Ah, me! it's a wicked world, and when a clever man turns his brain to crime it is the worst of all. I think that I have seen enough now, Miss Stoner, and, with your permission, we shall walk out upon the lawn.'

I had never seen my friend's face so grim or his brow so dark, as it was when we turned from the scene of this investigation. We had walked several times up and down the lawn, neither Miss Stoner nor myself liking to break in upon his thoughts before he roused himself from his reverie.

'It is very essential, Miss Stoner,' said he, 'that you should absolutely follow my advice in every respect.'

'I shall most certainly do so.'

'The matter is too serious for any hesitation. Your life may depend upon your compliance.'

'I assure you that I am in your hands.'

'In the first place, both my friend and I must spend the night in your room.'

Both Miss Stoner and I gazed at him in astonishment.

'Yes, it must be so. Let me explain. I believe that that is the village inn over there?'

'Yes, that is the "Crown."'

'Very good. Your windows would be visible from there?'

'Certainly.'

'You must confine yourself to your room, on pretence of a headache, when your stepfather comes back. Then when you hear him retire for the night, you must open the shutters of your window, undo the hasp, put your lamp there as a signal to us, and then withdraw with everything which you are likely to want into the room which you used to occupy. I have no doubt that, in spite of the repairs, you could manage there for one night.'

'Oh, yes, easily.'

'The rest you will leave in our hands.'

'But what will you do?'

'We shall spend the night in your room, and we shall investigate the cause of this noise which has disturbed you.'

'I believe, Mr Holmes, that you have already made up your mind,' said Miss Stoner, laying her hand upon my companion's sleeve.

'Perhaps I have.'

Then for pity's sake tell me what was the cause of my sister's death.'

'I should prefer to have clearer proofs before I speak.'

'You can at least tell me whether my own thought is correct, and if she died from some sudden fright.'

'No, I do not think so. I think that there was probably some more tangible cause. And now, Miss Stoner, we must leave you, for if Dr Roylott returned and saw us, our journey would be in vain. Goodbye, and be brave, for if you will do what I have told you, you may rest assured that we shall soon drive away the danger that threatens you.'

Sherlock Holmes and I had no difficulty in engaging a bedroom and sitting-room at the Crown Inn. They were on the upper floor, and from our window we could command a view of the avenue gate, and of the inhabitated wing of Stoke Moran manor house. At dusk we saw Dr Grimesby Roylott drive past, his huge form looming up beside the little figure of the lad who drove him. The boy had some slight difficulty in undoing the heavy iron gates, and we heard the hoarse roar of the Doctor's voice, and saw the fury with which he shook his clenched fists at him. The trap drove on, and a few minutes later we saw a sudden light spring up among the trees as the lamp was lit in one of the sitting-rooms.

'Do you know, Watson,' said Holmes, as we sat together in the gathering darkness, 'I have really some scruples as to taking you tonight. There is a distinct element of danger.'

'Can I be of assistance?'

'Your presence might be invaluable.'

'Then I shall certainly come.'

'It is very kind of you.'

'You speak of danger. You have evidently seen more in these rooms than was visible to me.'

'No, but I fancy that I may have deduced a little more. I imagine that you saw all that I did.'

'I saw nothing remarkable save the bell-rope, and what purpose that could answer I confess is more than I can imagine.'

'You saw the ventilator, too?'

'Yes, but I do not think that it is such a very unusual thing to have a small opening between two rooms. It was so small that a rat could hardly pass through.'

'I knew that we should find a ventilator before ever we came to Stoke Moran.'

'My dear Holmes!'

'Oh, yes, I did. You remember in her statement she said that her sister could smell Dr Roylott's cigar. Now, of course, that suggests at once that there must be a communication between the two rooms. It could only be a small one, or it would have been remarked upon at the coroner's inquiry. I deduced a ventilator.'

'But what harm can there be in that?'

'Well, there is at least a curious coincidence of dates. A ventilator is made, a cord is hung, and a lady who sleeps in the bed dies. Does not that strike you?'

'I cannot as yet see any connection.'

'Did you observe anything very peculiar about that bed?'

'No.'

'It was clamped to the floor. Did you ever see a bed fastened like that before?'

'I cannot say that I have'

'The lady could not move her bed. It must always be in the same relative position to the ventilator and to the rope - for so we may call it, since it was clearly never meant for a bell-pull.'

'Holmes,' I cried, 'I seem to see dimly what you are hitting at. We are only just in time to prevent some subtle and horrible crime.'

'Subtle enough and horrible enough. When a doctor does go wrong he is the first of criminals. He has nerve and he has knowledge. Palmer and Pritchard were among the heads of their profession. This man strikes even deeper, but I think, Watson, that we shall be able to strike deeper still. But we shall have horrors enough before the night is over: for goodness' sake let us have a quiet pipe, and turn our minds for a few hours to something more cheerful.'

About nine o'clock the light among the trees was extinguished, and all was dark in the direction of the manor house. Two hours passed slowly away, and then suddenly, just at the stroke of eleven, a single bright light shone out right in front of us.

'That is our signal,' said Holmes, springing to his feet; 'it comes from the middle window.'

As we passed out he exchanged a few words with the landlord, explaining that we were going on a late visit to an acquaintance, and that it was possible that we might spend the night there. A moment later we were out on the dark road, a chill wind blowing in our faces, and one yellow light twinkling in front of us through the gloom to guide us on our sombre errand.

There was little difficulty in entering the grounds, for unrepaired breaches gaped in the old park wall. Making our way among the trees, we reached the lawn, crossed it, and were about to enter through the window, when out from a clump of laurel bushes there darted what seemed to be a hideous and distorted child, who threw itself on the grass with writhing limbs, and then ran swiftly across the lawn into the darkness.

'My God!' I whispered, 'did you see it?'

Holmes was for the moment as startled as I. His hand closed like a vice upon my wrist in his agitation. Then he broke into a low laugh, and put his lips to my ear.

'It is a nice household,' he murmured, 'that is the baboon.'

I had forgotten the strange pets which the Doctor affected. There was a cheetah, too; perhaps we might find it upon our shoulders at any moment. I confess that I felt easier in my mind when, after following Holmes's example and slipping off my shoes, I found myself inside the bedroom. My companion noiselessly closed the shutters, moved the lamp on to the table, and cast his eyes round the room. All was as we had seen it in the day-time. Then, creeping up to me and making a trumpet of his hand, he whispered into my ear again so gently that it was all that I could do to distinguish the words:

'The least sound would be fatal to our plans.'

I nodded to show that I had heard.

'We must sit without a light. He would see it through the ventilator.'

I nodded again.

'Do not go to sleep; your very life may depend upon it. Have your pistol ready in case we should need it. I will sit on the side of the bed, and you in that chair.'

I took out my revolver and laid it on the corner of the table.

Holmes had brought up a long thin cane, and this he placed upon the bed beside him. By it he laid the box of matches, and the stump of a candle. Then he turned down the lamp and we were left in darkness.

How shall I ever forget that dreadful vigil! I could not hear a sound, not even the drawing of a breath, and yet I knew that my companion sat open-eyed, within a few feet of me, in the same state of nervous tension in which I was myself. The shutters cut off the least ray of light, and we waited in absolute darkness. From outside came the occasional cry of a night-bird, and once at our very window a long drawn, cat-like whine, which told us that the cheetah was indeed at liberty. Far away we could hear the deep tones of the parish clock, which boomed out every quarter of an hour. How long they seemed, those quarters! Twelve o'clock, and one, and two, and three, and still we sat waiting silently for whatever might befall.

Suddenly there was the momentary gleam of light up in the direction of the ventilator, which vanished immediately, about was succeeded by a strong smell of burning oil and heated metal. Someone in the next room had lit a dark lantern. I heard a gentle sound of movement, and then all was silent once more, though the smell grew stronger. For half an hour I sat with straining ears. Then suddenly another sound became audible-a very gentle, soothing sound, like that of a small jet of steam escaping continually from a kettle. The instant that we heard it, Holmes sprang from the bed, struck a match, and lashed furiously with his cane at the bell-pull.

'You see it, Watson?' he yelled. 'You see it?'

But I saw nothing. At the moment when Holmes struck the light I heard a low, clear whistle, but the sudden glare flashing into my weary eyes made it impossible for me to tell what it was at which my friend lashed so savagely. I could, however, see that his face was deadly pale, and filled with horror and loathing.

He had ceased to strike, and was gazing up at the ventilator, when suddenly there broke from the silence of the night the most horrible cry to which I have ever listened. It swelled up louder and louder, a hoarse yell of pain and fear and anger all mingled in the one dreadful shriek. They say that away down in the village, and even in the distant parsonage, that cry raised the sleepers from their beds. It struck cold to our hearts, and I stood gazing at Holmes, and he at me, until the last echoes of it had died away into the silence from which it rose.

'What can it mean?' I gasped.

'It means that it is all over,' Holmes answered. 'And perhaps, after all, it is for the best. Take your pistol and we shall enter Dr Roylott's room.'

With a grave face he lit the lamp, and led the way down the corridor. Twice he struck at the chamber door without any reply from within. Then he turned the handle and entered, I at his heels, with the cocked pistol in my hand.

It was a singular sight which met our eyes. On the table stood a dark lantern with the shutter half open, throwing a brilliant beam of light upon the iron safe, the door of which was ajar. Beside this table, on the wooden chair, sat Dr Grimesby Roylott, clad in a long grey dressing-gown, his bare ankles protruding beneath, and his feet thrust into red heelless Turkish slippers. Across his lap lay the short stock with the long lash which we had noticed during the day. His chin was cocked upwards, and his eyes were fixed in a dreadful rigid stare at the corner of the ceiling. Round his brow he had a peculiar yellow band, with brownish speckles, which seemed to be bound tightly round his head. As we entered he made neither sound nor motion.

The band! the speckled band!' whispered Holmes.

I took a step forward, In an instant his strange headgear began to move, and there reared itself from among his hair the squat diamond-shaped head and puffed neck of a loathsome serpent.

'It was a swamp adder!' cried Holmes - 'the deadliest snake in India. He has died within ten seconds of being bitten. Violence does, in truth recoil upon the violent, and the schemer falls into the pit which he digs for another. Let us thrust this creature back into its den, and we can then remove Miss Stoner to some place of shelter, and let the county police know what has happened.'

As he spake he drew the dog whip swiftly from the dead man's lap, and throwing the noose round the reptile's neck, he drew it from its horrid perch, and carrying it at arm's length, threw it into the iron safe, which he closed upon it.

Such are the true facts of the death of Dr Grimesby Roylott, of Stoke Moran. It is not necessary that I should prolong a narrative which has already run to too great a length, by telling how we broke the sad news to the terrified girl, how we conveyed her by the morning train to the care of her good aunt at Harrow, of how the slow process of official inquiry came to the conclusion that the doctor met his fate while indiscreetly playing with a dangerous pet. The little which I had yet to learn of the case was told me by Sherlock Holmes as we travelled back next day.

'I had,' said he, 'come to an entirely erroneous conclusion, which shows, my dear Watson, how dangerous it always is to reason from insufficient data.

The presence of the gipsies, and the use of the word "band," which was used by the poor girl, no doubt, to explain the appearance which she had caught a horrid glimpse of by the light of her match, were sufficient to put me upon an entirely wrong scent. I can only claim the merit that I instantly reconsidered my position when, however, it became clear to me that whatever danger threatened an occupant of the room could not come either from the window or the door. My attention was speedily drawn, as I have already remarked to you, to this ventilator, and to the bell-rope which hung down to the bed. The discovery that this was a dummy, and that the bed was clamped to the floor, instantly gave rise to the suspicion that the rope was there as a bridge for something passing through the hole, and coming to the bed.

The idea of a snake instantly occurred to me, and when I coupled it with my knowledge that the Doctor was furnished with a supply of creatures from India, I felt that I was probably on the right track. The idea of using a form of poison which could not possibly be discovered by any chemical test was just such a one as would occur to a clever and ruthless man who had had an Eastern training. The rapidity with which such a poison would take effect would also, from his point of view, be an advantage. It would be a sharp-eyed coroner indeed who could distinguish the two little dark punctures which would show where the poison fangs had done their work. Then I thought of the whistle. Of course, he must recall the snake before the morning light revealed it to the victim. He had trained it, probably by the use of the milk which we saw, to return to him when summoned. He wuld put it through the ventilator at the hour that he thought best, with the certainty that it would crawl down the rope, and land on the bed. It might or might not bite the occupant, perhaps she might escape every night for a week, but sooner or later she must fall a victim.

'I had come to these conclusions before ever I had entered his room. An inspection of his chair showed me that he had been in the habit of standing on it, which, of course, would be necessary in order that he should reach the ventilator. The sight of the safe, the saucer of milk, and the loop of whipcord was enough to finally dispel any doubts which may have remained. The metallic clang heard by Miss Stoner was obviously caused by her father hastily closing the door of his safe upon its terrible occupant. Having once made up my mind, you know the steps which I took in order to put the matter to the proof. I heard the creature hiss, as I have no doubt that you did also, and I instantly lit the light and attacked it.'

'With the result of driving it through the ventilator.'

'And also with the result of causing it to turn upon its master at the other side. Some of the blows of my cane came home, and roused its snakish temper, so that it flew upon the first person it saw. In this way I am no doubt indirectly responsible for Dr Grimesby Roylott's death, and I cannot say that it is likely to weigh very heavily upon my conscience.'